Wolcott Calkins

Memorial of Matthias W. Baldwin

Wolcott Calkins

Memorial of Matthias W. Baldwin

ISBN/EAN: 9783337093662

Printed in Europe, USA, Canada, Australia, Japan

Cover: Foto ©Raphael Reischuk / pixelio.de

More available books at **www.hansebooks.com**

MEMORIAL

OF

MATTHIAS W. BALDWIN.

"DO GOOD BY STEALTH, AND BLUSH TO FIND IT FAME."

PHILADELPHIA:
PRIVATELY PRINTED
1867.

COLLINS, PRINTER,
705 JAYNE ST.

CONTENTS.

MEMORIAL.

MEMORIAL.

It is no part of the purpose of this volume to perpetuate the painful recollections of a bereavement already severely deplored. We may leave to the unbelieving world that long bewildered anguish for the departed which receives no consolation from religion. This life is their only life; as its loss is irreparable, their mourning for death may well be without bounds; as they have no hope beyond the grave, time may obliterate, but can never relieve their desolation. But to the Christian there is not only a time to weep, but a measure to tears. To restrain the first impulses of grief for such a loss as we have suffered would be doing violence to our nature; but to cherish these feelings for the sake of that mysterious luxury which despondency affords, would be a denial of the sublimest truths of our religion. The same graces of character which cause us to regret the

2

death of the righteous invite us to rejoice in
their felicity, and hope for their resurrection
and life everlasting.

Nor does it enter into the design of this memorial to compose a worthy eulogy of the character of our departed friend. He needs no
words of praise. The grateful recollections of
thousands whom he has benefited, and the enduring monuments of his beneficence which
adorn the city where he spent his life, constitute
his best eulogy. And besides, it is in vain that
we attempt to honor the memory of the departed, if we do not calmly consider and firmly follow the Christian graces which have adorned
their conversation in this world, and cheered
their entrance to the next with the hopes of an
inheritance incorruptible, undefiled, that fadeth
not away.

But it is believed that there are materials for
thoughtful study in the life of a man who has
risen to be the head of one of the largest manufacturing establishments in the country; who is
indebted for his success neither to artifice nor
fortune, but to his own exertions alone; who
has never violated a principle of honor nor com-
promised a precept of religion in any business

transaction; who has not suffered his own prejudices nor his interests to turn him aside from
the path of rectitude; who has served the city
and the State and the Church in positions of
immense responsibility, and in times of perilous
excitement, and always in defence of right principles, at personal sacrifice; who has received
from the Fountain of infinite goodness a disposition to employ his fortune and influence in
works of illustrious beneficence; and who has
distinguished himself beyond all who have preceded him in his own peculiar vocation, by
making it his unalterable purpose to fight his
good fight and finish his course while living,
and not rely upon uncertain legacies to make
good the defects of a half-consecrated life.

The early struggles and unceasing labors for
the attainment of these high ends, are now the
priceless recollections of a few persons who
must soon join him in another world. It is the
design of this sketch to gather up these treasures
faithfully, and weave them into a narrative which
will be read with interest by a large circle of
friends, who may be safely invited to imitate
this beautiful life.

THE gracious providence of God has always prepared those who are to serve Him in positions of great responsibility and peculiar difficulties, by an early training corresponding to their destiny. The birth and education of MATTHIAS WILLIAM BALDWIN appear to have been adjusted by Infinite Wisdom to the influence he was called to exert on this community.

He was born in Elizabethtown, New Jersey, the tenth day of December, A. D. 1795. His father, William Baldwin, was a member of the Presbyterian church of Elizabethtown, and greatly beloved in every relation of life. He supported his family comfortably by the business of carriage making, and left them a considerable property at his death; but this was almost entirely lost subsequently by the bad management of the executors, and the widow was left to her own exertions with a family of five children, Matthias, the youngest, being four years old. This apparent disaster may have been the provi-

dential beginning of his fortunes and his character. It gave him an example of thrift,
ingenuity, and independence, the influence of
which may be traced through his whole career.
For his mother was a remarkable woman. By
indefatigable industry she kept her little family
together, afforded them fair advantages, and
superintended their education herself.

In his boyhood he had little taste for reading
or study. He enjoyed average advantages for
education, but never in his youth fixed his attention with any great persistence or zeal upon
books. The bent of his mind, from his earliest
years, was toward mechanical contrivances. The
toys he usually played with were those which
he himself had made. If he received one as a
present, he would take it to pieces to learn its
construction. The abilities of his father, who
was an excellent mechanic, and the genius of
his mother, seem to have been combined in this
child, and the beginning of his brilliant career
in the useful arts was made in his mother's cot-
tage. He turned her rooms into workshops.
He scattered whittlings and filings everywhere.
While his hands were busy in assisting his mo-

ther at her work, his mind was occupied in inventing some labor-saving machine.

Very few incidents in his childhood are remembered by his survivors. The following is recorded, not so much from anything remarkable in itself, as for the interest it derives from his sterling honesty through all the vicissitudes of his subsequent life. His incessant labors upon miniature toys and machines naturally consumed a great deal of material. On returning from school one day with a companion, they passed a new building which was just receiving its roof. A pile of new white pine shingles, made by the old process of shaving, lay in their path. What a temptation to whittling boys! Surprise at their moderation will be the only emotion upon learning that they each took but one. Matthias carried his directly to his mother, and told her where he found it, and what he was going to make of it. But she soon dispelled his vision of water-wheels and wind-mills, and made him reproach himself as bitterly as if he had committed a really grave offence. That was a sad evening in the widow's home. The boy cried as if his heart would break. The mother and sisters soon lost their severity in judging the offender, in sympathy for his distress. They had no peace till of his own accord he carried the shingle back and obtained forgiveness.

There is a lesson to be learned from the very slight records which can be made of these youthful days. Let boys follow the bent of their minds in things indifferent; curb them instantly where a moral principle is at stake. If Matthias' knives and gimlets and files had been taken away from him, and he had been confined at the indifferent schools of his native place, or sent away to better ones, the world would probably have lost a brilliant machinist, and might not have gained a distinguished scholar. But if his first encroachment upon the laws of property had been overlooked, he might have lost that sensitiveness to honor which has since distinguished him more than all his inventions.

THE time had come when his love for mechanical tools was to be put to a better use than his own amusement. He could not bear to be dependent upon his mother any longer than was absolutely necessary, and he was determined to make himself master of some mechanical art. From the first the little toys of his construction had been remarkable for their finish. He was never content with a rough machine, which would do its work awkwardly. The finest materials were often called into requisition, and received at his hands a marvellous polish. He had often inspected for hours the mechanism of the watch, and the height of his ambition was to understand its complicated structure. This natural taste, and a favorable opening, decided the nature of his first employment At the age of sixteen he was apprenticed to the Woolworth Brothers, in Frankford, Philadelphia County, to learn the trade of a jeweller. During the five years of his apprenticeship his life passed quietly, without incident of any interest to the public. He enjoyed a home in the family of one of his employers. He was also introduced to other excellent families of the place, and formed intimacies which were precious to him through life. He made himself singular among the young men of his acquaintance by refusing to indulge in any intoxicating drinks. A dreadful example of intemperance in a relative of his father's seemed to be constantly before his eyes; and he commenced life with the principle which he always followed, of total abstinence. His remarkable taste for music was also developed at this period; and his highest enjoyment was the social meetings of the little Presbyterian church for the practice of sacred song.

While he was thus employed his mother had moved to Philadelphia, and in the early part of 1817 he entered the establishment of Fletcher and Gardener, 130 Chestnut Street, where the Western National Bank now stands. They were extensive manufacturers of jewelry, and were obliged to repose great confidence in their journeymen. Mr. Baldwin soon became one of the most useful men in the shop. His work was not mere blind imitation. He loved to make a

3

perfect thing. He was too conscientious to
venture upon hazardous experiments, yet the
frequent orders demanding thought, taste, and
invention, soon began to pass into his hands.
He was enthusiastic in work which others performed as a mere routine. He thus rose rapidly
in the esteem of his employers, and yet never
lost the confidence and even affection of his fellow workmen. With them he was rather reti-
cent, yet always genial and cheerful.

But he was independent also, and just as determined in what he felt to be right, as if he had
been the proprietor of the whole establishment.
Many traits of character which have since become prominent, were noticed at this early
day. All his acquaintances have observed, for
example, his firmness of purpose, which often
seemed to verge rather close upon obstinacy.
He had a way which was quite provoking sometimes, of doing just what he thought right,
without appearing to listen to the very decided
protests of friends. It came to be pretty well
understood at last, that words were thrown away
after he had once made up his mind. This
disposition had some rough tests at this period.
He was using a tool one day which a fellow

journeyman claimed, and was about to transfer to his own bench. Baldwin looked at it carefully, and replied—

"That tool is mine."

Then commenced a war of words all on one side. His neighbor proved to his own satisfaction, by a variety of arguments, that the article belonged to him. Not a word from Baldwin. He kept quietly on with his work. But the moment an attempt was made to take the tool, a contest began which effectually prevented all attempts to trifle with him in the future.

He worked as a journeyman two years. His wages were considered excellent then, and his life was free from care, and full of bright expectations. He has often dwelt upon the recollections of those early days with the liveliest pleasure. His labors upon objects of exquisite beauty developed his taste for art, and he always took the path to and from his shop which led him by the windows where the finest paintings and engravings were exposed. Then he would sit by his fireside in the delicious repose which only hard work and a good conscience can impart, and dream of the time when his home would be full of the beautiful things he loved, and he would give poor journeymen something better to look at than the windows of print stores.   He lived to do noble things, as well as dream them.

By close economy, which was seconded at home with interest, and by the help of some capital from the same source, he was able to commence the manufacture of ornamental jewelry in a small way, in 1819. His reputation as an honest and ingenious workman attracted custom immediately, and his success was very flattering. Opportunities for working out original ideas of his own were now afforded, and eagerly followed. He seemed to be just beginning to realize his most ardent expectations, when, by a curious revulsion known to all the trades, jewelry seemed to go literally out of fashion. There was no demand even for such excellent and tasteful work as his. He was thus arrested at the very beginning of his career in an employment for which he had made such laborious preparations. Providence had something better for him to do!

Still his apprenticeship and four years' employment in this trade were not lost, but proved

to be the best possible preparation for his labors
of surpassing usefulness in after life. Their
influence may be traced in two remarkable traits
of his character as a machinist: First, the minute accuracy and perfect finish of all his work.
This was unquestionably the result of his experiments with the finer metals at that period, and
the master hand he acquired with the engraver's
tools. In fact he produced a finish which required better tools than could then be purchased.
He has often said that his manufacturing was a
work of necessity. He was never engaged in a
business in his life which did not demand finer
machines than he could buy. He was never
content to imitate others blindly. He not only
made progress in every art, but paved the way
for his progress from the beginning. Secondly,
his work upon jewelry was a stimulus, and at
the same time a safeguard to his inventive spirit.
It is remarkable that a man of such marvellous
ingenuity wasted so little of his life on chi-
merical inventions. The Patent Office is full
of magnificent follies; the creations of fertile
brains, without the balance of a thorough scientific training. Mr. Baldwin was then ignorant
of theoretical science; he had not pursued the

study of pure mathematics, chemistry, nor me-
tallurgy. But in the place of the restraint imposed by a scientific training, he had the drill
of a long and tedious apprenticeship, with a
thoroughly practical knowledge of all materials
employed in the arts. He was equally eminent,
therefore, in sagacity and courage. The inventions which he made at this period justify this
estimate of him as fully as those which are better known to the public.

One of them was a new process of Gold
Plating, which was never protected by a patent,
and is now very generally employed. Instead
of attaching the gold leaf to the baser metal,
he soldered a thicker piece of gold to the base,
and rolled the two together until they were
compressed to the required thinness.

His love for these pursuits, which survived
the impetuous spirit of youth, and supplied his
later years with recreations, was a motive of a
very high order in all his labors. Ingenuity,
natural genius, and original invention filled his
mind with that glowing enthusiasm which lifted
him above the routine of reluctant toil into the
region of adventurous exploit. He was more
than artisan—always artist.

He was thus prepared for more useful work than making articles for personal adornment, just when this employment ceased to be profitable. But God was not only guiding his steps, but touching his conscience. The decreasing demand for jewelry, his successful experiments with steel, and his bold spirit of adventure, may have had something to do in his change of employment. But we have the most unquestionable evidence that the decisive consideration after all, was a scruple of conscience. One of the very few revelations of his secret purposes which he ever made in conversation, refers to this period, and expresses in the energetic language which he knew how to use, the actual reasons which induced him to "put away childish things."

"One night I sat down to think my life over," he said, "and what account I should give in the day of judgment, for all my labors; and I made up my mind I could not bear to say I had spent my time *in making gewgaws!*" This was many years before he professed to be a Christian.

THE special providence of God is a truth so
constantly revealed in the life of every man,
that an honest doubt of it would seem to be
impossible. The experience of all good men
at least goes to prove that God never suffers a
reasonable scruple to weigh upon the conscience
without providing the means to obey it instantly.
Mr. Baldwin's life is full of examples of this
kind. One of the most instructive among them
occurred at this time.

Just when his conscience, his tastes, and the
exigency of his business demanded a career of
enlarged usefulness, the way was providentially
opened to him. He had often met a machinist
by the name of David Mason. This man was
now engaged in wood engraving, and had formed
an extensive acquaintance with the book pub-
lishers of the city. He observed that all their
tools and machines for binding were imported,
and conceived the idea of commencing the

4

manufacture of these articles himself. He proposed to share the business with Mr. Baldwin. They issued their circulars in the early part of 1825, and orders came in so rapidly that they soon gave up the employment in which they had each been engaged, and entered with zeal upon the new business. Their establishment was in a narrow street in the rear of Walnut, between Fourth and Fifth. In addition to the machines then in use, they manufactured hydraulic presses for binding. Through their bold enterprise the book trade became completely independent of the foreign market, and received valuable improvements. The most ingenious and beautiful designs for stamping the gilt lettering upon the backs and covers of books were produced from their shop. The stiff and gloomy appearance of library shelves began to give place to wreaths and rosettes and leaves, surrounding the attractive titles. Rev. Albert Barnes still retains as a precious memento of his lifelong friend—a little stamp, containing the watchword of his studies, "BIBLE," wreathed in a lacework of delicate vines. Mr. Baldwin's designs were remarkably chaste and appropriate.

To this they soon added the manufacture of

cylinders for printing calicoes. The figures or devices to be impressed upon the cloth were engraved upon the surface of these rollers, instead of plane blocks as formerly, and the whole piece of muslin passed through the press in a continuous motion. Various methods were tried to diminish the hand labor required in the preparation of these cylinders, such as etching and punching the surface of the copper with tools previously containing the proposed device. But the best tool for this purpose proved to be a little roller called a "mill." This was a few inches long and less than an inch in diameter, and the required device being once engraved on its surface, could be transferred to the cylinder by rolling. But Mr. Baldwin was not content with this. He was determined to diminish the manual labor in preparing these "mills." He had previously experimented upon dies for bank-note printing, and had succeeded in producing a facsimile of a die upon another piece of steel, by pressure alone. The original die was impressed upon a surface of soft steel, this was then hardened and impressed upon another, which last reproduced with mathematical precision the features of the original die. This invention was certainly original with Mr. Baldwin, though others may have employed it before him, and we find no claim on his part to a patent, and no evidence that he ever carried on the business of bank-note engraving. But the application of the same principle to the preparation of copper cylinders for printing calico was one of his most remarkable discoveries, and deserves to be ranked along with stereotyping, in its kindred art. The former method of making these mills was by punches. The punches having on them the required device, were driven into the roller, and the metal raised up was faced off, and the parts united and trimmed with a graver; a process which required so much hand work that the whole figure was often cut in with a graver in preference. The improvement of Mason and Baldwin consisted in *etching* the device on the steel mill. By covering the steel surface with a varnish or etching ground, tracing upon this the required figure, and plunging the whole into an acid prepared in a peculiar manner, he succeeded in etching upon soft steel as perfectly as upon copper. A few touches of the graver would finish the device, and no more work by hand would be required for the whole copper cylinder. For this "mill," being hardened, was rolled with immense pressure upon another of precisely the same dimensions, which thus presented the same figures in relief. This second steel cylinder was then in turn hardened, and rolled with the same pressure upon the surface of the large printing cylinder of copper. By the time the copper cylinder had made one revolution, the faithful little die had made repeated indentations of the designs to be produced upon the fabric with surprising accuracy. It then only required readjustment, and another revolution would impress the same figures by the side of the first. The process was continued until the whole cylinder was ready for use without a touch from the engraver's hand! The dies were preserved, and the plates with all their matchless perfection could be multiplied indefinitely.*

Engraving has made such advances since that day, and Mr. Baldwin's own achievements have been so much more brilliant, that this success is almost forgotten except by the few who remember the incredulity it encountered when he first proposed it, and the astonishment with which

* Journal Franklin Institute, June, 1828, p. 418.

its success was received. It made a complete revolution in this branch of our manufacturing interests, then just rising to importance. It is gratifying to know, also, that it was the beginning of his own prosperity. He often sat down to his work upon the little mill, and earned thirty dollars before rising from his seat. New difficulties were encountered and successively overcome. More colors than one were required. He made cylinders for printing in three different colors, mounted them in frames, and finished the complete machines for this difficult process.

The "gewgaws" have already been supplanted by works of great usefulness. He has fashioned a delicate and attractive binding for the volume of God's word. The millions of mothers and sisters who have to struggle in the brave way he had always witnessed at home, he has provided with cheap and elegant garments. He has left the political parties to wrangle about the United States Bank and the tariffs, while he has been quietly arresting the exportation of cotton, and increasing home manufactures. And by thus following a principle of conscience, he has laid the foundation for enduring prosperity, and provided himself a comfortable home.

He was by no means wealthy at this time, yet his attention was directed to a better employment of his growing capital than the increase of his own comforts. A large number of apprentices and journeymen were now employed in his establishment, and he felt that they needed some better means of instruction in the mechanical arts than the city then afforded. The result of his deliberations with many men since eminent in science and industry, was the formation of the "Franklin Institute," which was incorporated March 30, 1824, the constitution having been adopted on the fifth of February. This admirable institution has offered instruction, models, drawings, and means for scientific experiment to multitudes of our rising mechanics; has preserved the only complete list of patents in the country, and has gathered the most valuable library in the city on the useful arts. Mr. Baldwin was an active member and liberal supporter of the institution from its origin. And the complete record of his successive inventions which its able journal contains, is a just tribute to his industry and ingenuity.

STATIONARY STEAM ENGINES.

The manufacture of the printing rollers increased the business of Mason & Baldwin to such an extent that the little establishment in "Bank Coffee-House Alley" soon became too narrow for the demands upon them, and their success warranted a considerable enlargement. Near the close of 1827 or early in 1828 they removed to Minor Street, designing to continue the same business. But the time had now come for Mr. Baldwin to enter upon the great work of his life. The increasing facilities of the new shop made the old hand machines and foot lathes intolerable. Horse power was tried and proved wholly inadequate. At last a steam-engine was purchased, the best which was then to be obtained. But Mr. Baldwin was dissatisfied with its performance, and after a few attempts to improve it, decided to manufacture a new one after original drawings of his own. This was a compact little engine of about five horse power, upright, and occupying a space of about six square feet. So perfect was the construction of every part that it was absolutely noiseless in its motion. It stood near the entrance of the shop, and the opening door entirely hid it from view, so that visitors seeing nothing and hearing nothing, inquired with wonder where the power came from. The boiler was beneath, near the forge of the blacksmith, who supplied the fuel.

This little engine is still in use, with scarcely diminished powers, at the advanced age of nearly forty years. It drives the machinery of the whole boiler shop in the Broad Street factory. A friend of Mr. Baldwin, of some antiquarian tastes, visited the venerable relic since his death, and asked the engineer why they did not relieve it of these arduous labors in order to prolong its existence.

"I used to ask Mr. Baldwin," he replied, "to ease her up a little. But he said he meant to do all the work he could as long as he lived, and he required as much of his machines."

This engine was not only more complete in finish and powerful in movement than any which had preceded it in this country, but contained an original invention of the greatest importance in marine engineering. To convert the horizontal motion of the piston into rotary motion, requires a connecting rod which can move with the crank of the fly wheel. This rod is usually attached to the extremity of the piston, so that the revolving shaft must be removed from the cylinder the whole length of both piston and connecting rod. Mr. Baldwin set his cylinder upright; fixed the end of the piston into a kind of frame like the gate of a saw-mill, which was attached to the cylinder by guides on each side, and played up and down in the same space. Another gate outside of this, attached to it at the bottom, and vibrating freely at the top, gave motion to the crank. The whole machine was thus compressed into half the space usually occupied. This invention, called for to economize room in the Minor Street shop, contains in a germ the principles of the ponderous engines of our steamships.

The religious public will be interested to know the use to which the second engine of Mr. Baldwin's construction was put. It was a little five-horse machine for the American Sunday-School Union. The first Christian literature for the young ever printed in America by steam, was probably the work of this engine. He has been Superintendent of Sabbath-Schools since; he has built many mission chapels; but his first work for the children was furnishing their beautiful books by the thousands.

The manufacture of stationary engines soon became the most important business of the shop. And their increased power created a demand which stimulated competition. A stranger came to him one day with excellent introductions, and after a moment's general conversation, made known his errand. He told him candidly that he was going into business in opposition to him, and as the superiority of the Baldwin engines consisted in the excellence of his materials, and the perfect make of his boilers, he asked him if he was willing to inform him where he obtained his iron, and who made his boilers. Mr. Baldwin gave him the desired information without a moment's hesitation, with the generous remark that there was room enough for them both.

The business now became so large as to alarm the timid and cautious Mason. He therefore withdrew from the firm in a year or two after the Minor Street property was purchased. But

Mr. Baldwin had the confidence of the hands to such a degree, that every man remained with him and the work went on without the slightest interruption.

The review of these ten years is full of suggestion to young men of enterprise and integrity. The industrious and faithful apprentice has been a journeyman, and an independent manufacturer. He has invented machines which increase tenfold the capacity of labor. He has introduced into this country two or three new articles of manufacture which are increasing immensely its material interests. He has assisted in founding an institution which will develop the character and make the fortune of whole generations of young men yet unborn. And now he has become one of the foremost manufacturers of stationary steam engines in America. All this in ten years, with half of his threescore and ten still to live!

THE GREAT CHANGE.

WE now come to the most important event in Mr. Baldwin's life. Our readers will probably anticipate the commencement of that magnificent enterprise which will always link his name on this side of the Atlantic with that of Stephenson in English history. But the building of the first locomotive was not to be compared with the event now to be described in its influence upon his own character and interests, much less in the good he has accomplished for others. Thus far he had been governed by principles of strict integrity. But a great change in worldly prosperity was just before him. He was soon to be tried by such success as few men have endured without corruption. He was to be brought into competition with men who would gladly turn his principles against him, to ruin the enterprise on which his reputation and his success depended. He was to encounter temptations to seek his own aggrandizement by methods which all the world would applaud.

Opportunities were now to open before him, to
be one of the most selfish, or else one of the
most disinterested men in his generation. Had
he character enough for this trial? Would those
principles of simple justice and generosity to his
fellow men, carry him through this ordeal?

How often the experiment has been made;
how mournful the result has too often been!
It is not a conjecture, but an assurance of God's
word, that Mr. Baldwin would have failed in
the immense responsibilities now to be intrusted
to him, if he had received them with no other
principles in his heart than the love of honor,
and the generous disposition which had animated
him thus far. He had not been governed by
religious principle. He did not live a life of
prayer. He did not feel his dependence upon
God. He had amiable impulses, but he obeyed
them capriciously; he did not recognize the duty
of living for others rather than for himself. He
had no knowledge of God, and therefore no
true knowledge of himself nor of other men.
The essential narrowness of his purposes he had
never suspected, much less the buried energies
of his mind, and the capability of self-sacrifice
which were yet to be called to life.

All this birthright of his soul must be given to him by a painful struggle. We cannot see very clearly into the shadows which now deepened around him. He scarcely lifted the veil by a single word then, nor in all his subsequent life. We know the occasion. It was a quiet but solemn revival of religious interest in the Arch Street Church, where he worshipped. A young man of spare person, ungraceful gesture, but impassioned eloquence, breathing upon his crowded congregation the very spirit of his master, touched his soul to its profoundest depths.*

---

* Thomas H. Skinner, D.D., Professor in Union Theological Seminary, N. Y. The following letter will be an encouragement to ministers of the Gospel to "sow by all waters:"—

New York, Sept. 29, 1866.

Rev. and Dear Sir:

I did not know that the late M. W. Baldwin was converted under my preaching, and have no recollection of his religious experience, or any other acquaintance with his religious life, than what is common to the public. I have long held him in peculiar esteem, as a man of great excellence, and a evoted dservant of Christ, *and rejoice to bear through you, my* ministry *was the means of his conversion some forty years ago.* But I do not remember that I ever had a conversation with him on the subject of personal religion. His death is a great affliction, which I hope will be sanctified to his family and friends. He deserves a special memorial, and I am glad that you are engaged in preparing one, and regret that I cannot furnish you with the tribute you have requested of me.

With great regard, yours,

Thomas H. Skinner.

He was drawn by an influence which he made
no attempt to resist, into a meeting for personal
conversation.   Day after day for weeks, he
sought this and every means of grace.   But the
work was too thorough to be hastened.

He did not receive much help from conversation with Christians of experience.   As he
expressed it himself, in the revival of 1858,
Christians "did not use market language with
him; they did not make the gospel plain so that
common men could pick it up.   They fired over
his head.   They did not know how ignorant
sinners are."   For he soon got far enough to
feel himself a sinner.   He found that all his life
long, and not least in his proud self-reliance, his
heart was in defiant rebellion against God.   He
began to cry for mercy.   Behold, he prayeth!
Very soon, however, his prayers began to trouble
him.   He felt them to be such miserable ac-
knowledgments of mercies; such heartless con-
fessions of sins; such cold supplications for
forgiveness, that he seemed to be mocking rather
than worshipping God.   He went to an old
Christian and asked what he must do.

"Ask for grace," was the reply.

Again he got into trouble about temptation. Again he pressed the same inquiry.

"Ask for grace," was again the answer.

Once more he became embarrassed about duties, and receiving the same answer as before, he lost all patience, and exclaimed:—

"Why, one would think, according to you, that Christian life is nothing but *grace, grace, grace*, all the way through."

"And so IT IS," he lived to say in his old age. "All of grace" were almost the last words upon his lips. But he was too ignorant to understand it then.*

This little glimpse of his first religious experience, which he might not have afforded but for the hope of leading others to Him who said, "My grace is sufficient for thee," throws some light upon the nature of his struggle. Accustomed all his life to depend upon himself, it was hard for him to "cease from his own works" and "enter into rest." The spirit of childlike trust, which was the most beautiful characteristic of his piety in after life, was only imparted after

---

* Rev. George Duffield, jr., in *American Presbyterian*, Sept. 27, 1866.

he had tried his own strength to the utmost
and found it perfect weakness. He seemed to
fall like a wayward, wearied child, into the arms
of forgiving love, and to breathe out at once the
prayer and the assurance—

"Forever here my rest shall be."

Mr. Baldwin commenced his Christian life
with that directness and force which character-
ized all he ever undertook. He began in his
closet and very soon in his family. His first
prayer in the hearing of others will not soon be
forgotten. He did not dare to trust his own
words yet, and he availed himself of a simple
manual of family devotions. But one evening,
not long after, his prayer-book could not be
found. He looked in every room, and soon the
whole family joined in the search. But it was
lost. The children gathered round the fireside
with that curious awe which such a disaster was
calculated to inspire. Their wonder continued
till he had read the chapter to the close. Then
he kneeled down and commended them all to
the Heavenly Father, who knoweth what things
we have need of before we ask him. He never
used a prayer-book again.

Mr. Baldwin did not unite with the Church for several years after his conversion. About that time he became alienated from the Arch Street congregation by circumstances which show they little knew what a treasure they were losing. He found one Sabbath in the pew which he was occupying on brief rentals, a note with the statement, "This pew is sold, and must be vacated immediately." As no effort was made to find other sittings for his family, he inferred that he was not wanted there, and began to hear other ministers of the same denomination. He was led by curiosity to hear the newly-elected pastor of the First Church, on Washington Square. There was something in the simplicity, perspicuity, and straightforward earnestness of Mr. Barnes' preaching which completely captivated his heart.

In June, 1831, he was admitted to this church on confession of repentance and faith in the Saviour. He asked at once for labor in the vineyard. His first work was in the Sabbath School, where he taught successive classes, was then made Superintendent, and finally had a large Bible-class of young men, in the pastor's study. Elders of churches are still living who were converted in that Bible-class. For thirty-five years Mr. Baldwin was never absent, except by necessity, from the Sabbath School.

As an officer of the church in his later years, he was always remarkable for his eagerness to "bring the young men out" as soon as they joined the church. "I tell you," he used to say, "they never will do any good if they do not commence now." All this was a fruit of his own experience. No young Christian ever felt a greater shrinking from the duty of public prayer and conference. But from his conversion to his death he never paused to debate the question of performing a known duty. It never once occurred to him to consult his own feelings about doing the whole work of a Christian. And the prayer meeting felt the fervor of his piety from the very first.

Mr. Baldwin's conversion was a marked and thorough change of character. He was a whole-souled Christian from the first, and blended the spirit of childlike trust in God, which ever after formed such a beautiful element in his piety, with an immediate adjustment of his business to the Gospel standard of integrity, and the most aggressive labors in the cause of Christ.

The serenity of temper which has been so often attributed to his natural disposition, he has himself repeatedly ascribed to the grace of God overcoming the infirmities of an irritable nature. The conscience which always seemed to choose the right without thought or calculation, was not an instinct, but the gift of God in answer to prayer. His courage to defend righteous principles far in advance of his age, and illustrate them yet more conspicuously by his example, and his disposition to consecrate his wealth and influence to the good of others and the glory of God, were the fruits of this blessed experience of pure and undefiled religion. It would be an insufferable offence to his memory to hold up before the young his illustrious example without pointing them to the Fountain of infinite grace from which he derived his excellence. All the great moral qualities for which his name will be honored, date from about the time of his serious attention to personal religion.

LOCOMOTIVE BUILDING.

THE employment of steam for moving carriages on land had occupied the attention of inventors for nearly two centuries before it was successfully introduced into this country. Previous to 1641 Solomon de Caus conceived the idea, and came from Normandy to Paris to urge his design upon the king. He suffered for his temerity by a long imprisonment in the Bicêtre. The first actual model of a steam carriage of which we have any account was constructed by Cugnot, and exhibited before Marshal de Saxe in 1763. In 1769 a working steam carriage was constructed by the same man, which is still preserved in the Conservatoire des Arts et Métiers in Paris. But Richard Trevithick, a captain in a Cornish tin mine, has the honor of devising the first steam carriage actually used on common roads, in 1802. Some ten years later Mr. Blackett, of Wylan, introduced a locomotive upon a railroad constructed of wooden rails plated with cast iron.* These rude experiments paved the way for the successful introduction of steam power upon the English railways by George Stephenson. The engines of this remarkable inventor had been in operation more than ten years before any attempt was made to introduce them into this country. Still their success was not assured until 1827, when the exhaust steam from the cylinders was applied through a blast pipe into the chimney, to increase the draught of the furnace. This improvement increased the power of the machine to such an extent as to attract the attention of American railroad companies.

"The first locomotives in the United States were brought over from England by Horatio Allen, of New York, in the fall of 1829 or the spring of 1830; and one of them was set up on the Delaware and Hudson Railroad, at Carbondale, Pa., but being found too heavy for the track, its use was abandoned. The first locomotive constructed in this country was built by the West Point Foundry, at New York, in 1830, for the South Carolina Railroad, and named the

* Smiles' Life of Stephenson, chap. viii. Also, London Builder, No. 1148.

Phœnix; a second engine was built the same year, by the same establishment, and for the same road, and named the *West Point.* In the spring of 1831 a third engine was built by the same establishment, for the Mohawk and Hudson Railroad from Albany to Schenectady, and called the De Witt Clinton. This was the first locomotive run in the State of New York."*

In the fall of 1830, it was announced that the Camden and Amboy Railroad Company had imported a locomotive, which was jealously guarded from public inspection, in a storehouse near Philadelphia. Mr. Baldwin repaired to the spot at once with a friend, and by various devices overcame the scruples of the man in charge of the wonderful curiosity. He carefully observed the various parts of the machine, made a few furtive measurements, and at last crept under the ponderous boiler. Here he remained in absorbing study for nearly half an hour. As he emerged from his retreat his face was glowing with enthusiasm, and he exclaimed:

"I can make it!"

His companion was Franklin Peale, Esq., manager of the Philadelphia Museum, who had

---

* Journal Franklin Institute, May, 1858, p. 309.

felt so much confidence in his skill that he had given him previously an order for a working model. With no other assistance than this hurried inspection, and such drawings as the scientific journals of the day were publishing, he constructed a beautiful miniature locomotive, after the plan of Ericsson, since rendered famous by the Monitors. It was placed on a circular track in the Museum, April 25th, 1831, and attracted crowds of visitors.

His success with this model directed his attention to the bold undertaking of introducing upon American railroads a better locomotive than the few rude and unmanageable machines which were thus far employed. Early in 1832 he received an order from the Philadelphia and Germantown Railroad Company for one small locomotive. He abandoned the single upright cylinder of the Ericsson model, and introduced several other improvements which have proved of permanent value. His drawings were quite as original as if he had never seen a machine of the kind. His principal attention was directed to the apparatus for generating and economizing steam.

The whole work on this memorable pioneer

7

among American locomotives occupied about
six months. It was driven forward under a
pressure of difficulties which would have disheartened a less determined man. Not the least
of these was the lack of any place to do the
heavy forging. The only blacksmith shop in
the factory was in the cellar, and all the un-
wieldy work on the engine had to be done in
other establishments. While this experiment
was still in progress, he had contracted for a
more commodious building in Lodge Alley, between Seventh and Eighth Streets, with a considerable front on Market Street. He contrived
to move into the new place without losing a
day on his favorite work, and here the running
gears were attached and everything made ready
for the grand trial, which took place Nov. 23d,
1832.

The *United States Gazette* of the next day
contains the following editorial notice:—

"A most gratifying experiment was made
yesterday afternoon, on the Philadelphia, Germantown, and Norristown Railroad. The beautiful locomotive engine and tender, built by M.
W. Baldwin, of this city, whose reputation as
an ingenious machinist is well known, were for

the first time placed on the road. The engine travelled about six miles, working with perfect accuracy and ease in all its parts, and with great velocity."

A more extended notice appears in the *Chronicle* of the same date:—

"It gives us pleasure to state that the locomotive engine built by our townsman, M. W. Baldwin, has been proved highly successful. In the presence of several gentlemen of science and information on such subjects, the engine was yesterday placed upon the road for the first time. All her parts had been previously highly finished and fitted together in Mr. Baldwin's factory. She was taken apart on Tuesday, and removed to the Company's depot, and yesterday morning she was completely together, ready for travel. After the regular passenger cars had arrived from Germantown in the afternoon, the tracks being clear, preparation was made for her starting. The placing fire in the furnace and raising steam occupied twenty minutes. The engine (with her tender) moved from the depot in beautiful style, working with great ease and uniformity. She proceeded about half a mile beyond the Union Tavern, at the township line, and returned immediately, a distance of six miles, at a speed of about twenty-eight miles to the hour; her speed having been slackened at all the road crossings, and it being after dark, but a portion of her power was used. It is needless to say that the spectators were delighted. From this experiment there is every reason to believe this engine will draw thirty tons gross, at an average speed of forty miles an hour, on a level road. The principal superiority of the engine over any of the English ones known, consists in the light weight—which is but between four and five tons—her small bulk, and the simplicity of her working machinery. We rejoice at the result of this experiment, as it conclusively shows that Philadelphia, always famous for the skill of her mechanics, is enabled to produce steam engines for railroads combining so many superior qualities as to warrant the belief that her mechanics will hereafter supply nearly all the public works of this description in the country."

The following advertisement, which appeared in Poulson's *American Daily Advertiser*, Nov. 26, 1832, will be read with no little amusement:—

"NOTICE.—The locomotive engine (built by M. W. Baldwin, of this city) will depart daily *when the weather is fair*, with a train of passenger cars. *On rainy days horses will be attached!*"

But the triumph of that day was not to be unchallenged. No engineers in the country were prepared to run the new machine. There was only one man in the shop besides Mr. Baldwin who understood her construction well enough to make a successful trip with her. He was taken sick at the beginning of her career. Others were tried, and soon lost all patience with the intricate work. Day after day the President of the road, who insisted from the first that there were radical defects in the machine, threatened to condemn the work, and throw it back on Mr. Baldwin's hands. At last Mr. Pettit recovered, overhauled the abused machinery, and kept his place at the helm until she made regular trips, and gave fair satisfaction to her builder and purchasers.

The most contradictory statements are upon record in regard to the Ironsides. The papers of the day declare that she made a mile in fifty-seven seconds, a rate of over seventy miles an hour! Living witnesses insist that this is true, while others declare that the run was less than a mile, and occupied nearly two minutes. The truth probably lies between the two extremes. She was undoubtedly an imperfect machine, requiring important alterations and improvements, but still an honor to any machinist as a first experiment, and better adapted to her design than any other American locomotive of that date.

One of the very few moments of despondency in his whole life was occasioned by the ungracious reception awarded to this machine. In the spring of 1833, when he finally received three thousand five hundred dollars for his work ($500 less than the contract), he remarked to one of his apprentices with much decision: "that is our last locomotive." The remark was recalled to mind when the same apprentice, now an officer in the factory, happened to notice the No. 1500 on the engine erected at the time of Mr. Baldwin's death.

But other inventors were already in the field. A receipt on the books of the same Company shows that another engine, manufactured at the West Point Foundry, was purchased in April, 1833. And a very flattering notice of a locomotive named "Pennsylvania," constructed by Col. Long, of the U. S. Army, appears in the

Daily Chronicle of June 7th, 1833. The *Journal of the Franklin Institute* of the same year describes this machine as running on the Germantown Road at that time.

Whether this competition, or Mr. Baldwin's principles on Temperance and other reforms were prejudicial to his interests, cannot be now ascertained. But it is certain that he was eager for another trial long before he received his next order. Almost two years had intervened. Valuable improvements had been continually occurring to him. He was so impatient to set them in motion that he would have taken orders at almost any pecuniary loss. He would always insist upon working out his ideas at any cost. His next engine was in every respect a great improvement upon the Ironsides, and his reputation in this business was soon firmly established.

Very gradually the locomotive business began to assume the first importance in the shop, and to make even the immense building in Lodge Alley too contracted. Besides, it was almost impossible to remove the structure from the shop when completed.

In 1835, after some nine or ten locomotives had been completed here, the final move was made to Broad and Hamilton Streets. The new works were erected with a view to throwing the whole strength of the establishment into this one article of manufacture as speedily as possible.

This remarkable confidence, when there were few railroads and fewer locomotives in the country, was justified by the result. He continued to make stationary engines for several years in the new shop; and in 1837 he received the contract for the ponderous machinery of the city ice boat, which, amid difficulties of every kind, he finished so stanchly that they have worn out one hulk, and are just going, almost without repair, into another. But after this he began to decline all work, except upon his favorite locomotives.

The following are the principal improvements of Mr. Baldwin up to the year 1835. Some of them have not proved of permanent value, but they deserve to be placed on record, as suggestive experiments, and steps in the progress which placed him finally at the head of this magnificent enterprise in this country.

First: The guides of the piston were made hollow, and the cavities were used for the chambers of the force-pumps which supply water to the boiler; thus giving additional strength to the guides without much increase to their weight, and dispensing entirely with the frame and fixture of the ordinary force-pump. The facilities for removing and cleansing the valves, and preventing the danger of explosion, were also greatly increased.

Second: The motion of the steam-valves was reversed; the eccentrics were firmly secured to the axle, and less liable to get loose and out of repair. The treadle and its appendages, and no less than four rock-shafts, with the complicated head-gear of the English method, were entirely dispensed with. The rock-shafts which were retained and the eccentric banks were placed immediately under the eye and within the reach of the engineer.

Third: Instead of fixing the ends of the axle into the centres of the driving-wheels, he dispensed with one of the arms in each crank, and attached the wheel to the wrists of the crank, with its centre adjusted to the centre of the axle. The power of the engine was thus applied directly to the wheel, without the intervention of an arm of the crank, thus diminishing the

8

strain upon the axle, and lessening its liability to be broken, as also obviating the tendency of the driving-wheels to twist upon the axle and become loose; a very general and troublesome defect in previous engines. The distance between the two cranks was also thus increased about ten inches, which admitted of a corresponding enlargement of the boiler, and of a more advantageous disposition of the weight of the fire-place, by bringing it about fourteen inches nearer to the axle. This improvement has never been abandoned in engines which attach the connecting-rod to the inside of the wheel, and paved the way for the still greater enlargement of the boiler, and safety of the machinery, by the external attachment.

Fourth. The steam-pipe was introduced into the boiler through the opening by which it usually communicates between the dome and the cylinders. A twofold benefit resulted: (1.) The pipe could be made without a joint in the boiler. (2.) The "man-hole" in the boiler could be dispensed with; since the juncture between the dome and the boiler, as well as all other steam joints, being accurately fitted by grinding and formed without cement or packing, the dome could be easily taken off and replaced, and its aperture used for occasional access to the inside of the boiler.

Fifth. In the construction of the driving-wheels, the hubs and spokes were of iron, cast in one piece; felloes of hard wood were framed into the ends of the spokes, and the whole was firmly bound together by a stout tire of wrought iron, with a flange on its inner edge; thus by a judicious combination of iron and wood, the strength and firmness of the former were combined with the elasticity of the latter.*

* Journal of the Franklin Institute, April, 1835, p. 245.

Mr. Baldwin began his work upon locomotives about the time of uniting with the Christian Church. The increasing wealth and influence which the successive improvements we have now described afforded him, were religiously consecrated to the service of his Master. It has often been conjectured that his readiness to give industrious young men a hand to help them to independence, and his splendid works of charity, were in consequence of a disposition naturally generous. Worldly men would be reluctant to attribute to religion the whole of that beautiful life which they so greatly admired. But he has explicitly and repeatedly stated that the great work of systematic beneficence which he carried on through life, was all the result of God's grace in his heart. "I feel more thankful for the disposition to give largely, than for the ability to give largely," he often said; "for I know that immense wealth can be acquired a great deal easier than the heart to use it well. My money without a new heart would have been a curse to me."

It is also deeply affecting to know that the fountain of this grace was opened in his heart by a great sorrow. This is one of the very few incidents of a purely domestic character which delicacy to the living does not forbid to be recorded. In February, 1833, the little home in Tenth Street was gladdened by the birth of a bright healthy boy. Other sons were born and died in early infancy. But this seemed to be the child of promise. He passed the perils of his first year without an hour's sickness. And his opening character seemed to be as perfect as his constitution. He was one of those absolutely faultless children who always make loving hearts vacillate so painfully between anxiety and fascination. He was the pride and joy of his father. And he seemed associated in some way with his growing experience of Christ's love. He would often climb upon his lap in the morning, as he was reading the newspaper, and snatch it away indignantly and murmur—

"No, no, papa! Bible first! Bible first, papa!"

The good man would press the precious child to his heart with tears and thanksgivings for a little Samuel who seemed to hear the voice of God more clearly than himself.

For two sweet years, the happiest of his life, this new affection grew into his most sacred purposes. But one night in February, 1835, the child seemed restless; gasped for breath; the moisture dried upon his forehead; too soon it was evident that he was suffering with a severe attack of the croup. The father bent over him in speechless agony, and when he closed his eyes forever, the light of his own life seemed to go out too. There was silence and darkness in that home. Hampden was identified with everything. Labor, pleasure, and even religion, that last solace in sorrow, were all associated with the loved and lost. Day after day the Bible which he loved to hear papa read was opened, but tears hid the words of heavenly wisdom. He kneeled down, but missing the little head on which his hands used to rest, sobs choked his utterance. Every mention of the beloved name made him live over again all this anguish. At last they tacitly agreed to be silent. Not a word was ever breathed again in his presence of this overwhelming bereavement.

But the trial of his faith was precious. From

this experience of sorrow he came forth to his
work for the Master with a consecration of heart
he had never felt before. And the offering he
made in memory of Hampden was one of the
most beautiful charities of his life. Back of
his house was a little alley occupied by colored
families. Their children were growing up in
ignorance. He gathered them into a little
school, hired the rooms himself, and for years
supported the teachers. The privileges which
his son would never need were given to the
poor and the neglected. He took heed all his
life not to despise the little ones.

This school was only the beginning of Mr.
Baldwin's labors for this proscribed race. And
about the year 1835 an opportunity occurred for
enlisting the co-operation of others, and greatly
enlarging his usefulness. A colored man by the
name of Pompey Hunt was exerting a marked
influence on the people of his own color by the
natural eloquence peculiar to his race. He had
attracted the attention of several members of
Mr. Barnes' church, and at last they met to de-
vise means of raising the sum of two hundred
dollars a year to support Pompey and enable
him to give his whole time to Gospel labor.

They debated for an hour. The general tone was despondent. At last Mr. Baldwin took the floor:—

"Brethren, we have talked long enough. It is time something was done. We need not expect others to give unless we set them the example. I have laid aside twenty-five dollars for a new suit of clothes; but I can wear my old ones one winter longer. Put my name down for twenty-five."

This example of self-denial changed the spirit of the meeting in an instant. The paper went round again, and four hundred dollars were raised on the spot, and two city missionaries were employed instead of one.

This was the origin of the "Young Men's Missionary Association of the First Church." They engaged at once in the distribution of tracts, and the support of zealous laborers among the neglected population of the city. Mr. Baldwin is justly regarded as the Father of the Association, and its life and spirit from the beginning were owing to his own self-denying labors. He would never suffer an opportunity for doing good to be neglected for want of funds. "The Lord has opened the door. We must enter in. He will provide the means." Often he has given his note of hand for hundreds of dollars, when he could not contribute the cash. His friends remonstrated with him for this improvidence. But he always replied: "Nobody hesitates to sign promises to pay in the future, in order to get capital for business. Are we to trust the Lord to take care of our affairs, and not his own?" It was simple faith in God's promises which sustained him in this magnificent work of beneficence from the beginning. "Trust in the Lord and do good, and verily thou shalt be fed," he always felt to be a covenant with one who could not fail.

No member of that association will ever forget the feeling of admiration which thrilled their hearts when they received an unexpected contribution which had a peculiar history. It seems that after the crisis of 1837 business began to increase again, and the old liabilities were all fully redeemed, except one note which could not be found. After searching in every direction for it, Mr. Baldwin brought the amount, with interest calculated to the last cent, and paid it into the treasury of the Missionary Association, simply remarking that the money did

9

not belong to him, and as the rightful owner could not be found, he inferred that "the Lord had need of it."

The influence of the few simple words Mr. Baldwin would say on such occasions, and of his consistent example, was incalculable on the whole church. The habit of giving largely and systematically had not yet been formed in any of the churches. The most plain and earnest preaching upon this duty was comparatively fruitless, without a conspicuous example to enforce the Gospel truth. The example came in this instance from a comparatively poor man, who began his Christian life by following literally the commands of the Bible. This naturally excited jealousies, many misjudged his motives in surpassing so largely the contributions of those who were reputed rich. But they lived to believe him conscientious and perfectly unostentatious in this work. And his "zeal provoked many." His splendid munificence in after years did not exert such a marked influence on others as the constant self-denial of these years of comparative poverty. It is estimated by those who were intimately connected with him in this Association, that while he was living in the little Tenth Street house, which could have been rented for two or three hundred dollars, he was giving away ten thousand dollars a year! His benevolence then was actually a prejudice to his interest, when he needed financial assistance. Many refused to honor the drafts of a man who would make donations by promissory notes. But it is refreshing to record the fact that some of the banks of the city, and one in particular, took a more Christian view of the matter.

"You refuse to help him," said one president to another, "because he does not know what to do with his money. We will stand by him because he is determined to do good with his money. *His collaterals are God's promises!*"

The systematic plans of beneficence organized in this Association by Mr. Baldwin have been described more fully than his private charities because they are matters of public history, and illustrate his wisdom as well as his goodness of heart. But it must not be understood that these efforts were suffered to interfere with the daily appeals for the relief of suffering. This is a chapter in his life which can never be written. His most intimate friends know nothing of the immense sums which he has given away for this purpose in the course of his life. Indeed his own left hand never knew what his right hand was doing. He never could keep any money in his pocket. On arriving at his office in the morning, the first business was often to dispatch a clerk to pay the little debts he had contracted on the way up.

"Why, Mr. Baldwin!" he would exclaim, "why *do* you always run round the city without any money in your pocket?"

"Well, you see, I met my pastor on Chestnut Street with a Western Home Missionary, who wanted to get a little money to buy books for his library. I gave him all I had, only $50; little enough, I'm sure. Then I had a contract to sign at ———'s, and no money to secure it. You must hand him $5. I had to take a hack to the prison and back; the driver is waiting for his pay. And on the way back we passed a little girl bare-footed this cold weather. You must pay for the shoes and stockings I bought her at ———'s. What a blessing that my credit is good! They all seem willing to trust me, though I don't know them."

There was no such thing as keeping his bank

books in order. After everything had been
nicely balanced, donation checks from every
direction would begin to come in, which he
had forgotten. One day a gentleman came into
the Sabbath School of which Mr. Baldwin was
Superintendent, and approached him with an air
of familiarity, and asked the privilege of solicit-
ing contributions for an object which he had
much at heart.

"Who is that man?" asked Mr. Baldwin of
his pastor as soon as he could see him alone.

"Why, don't you know him? He says you
gave him $100 yesterday!"

"Ah, well! no wonder I had forgotten him;
there were a dozen of them at the office yesterday."

These private appeals became so numerous
that he was obliged to protect his repose at
home by making the rule that all applications
for charity must be made at his place of business. Still, the rule could bend sometimes, as
one example out of many will show. He was
awakened one cold winter night by violent ring-
ing at the door. As soon as he ascertained the
cause he dressed himself, and giving the shiver-
ing man who was waiting a warm overcoat,

went with him, carrying great baskets filled
with food and clothing. He found a family in
the neighborhood freezing and starving. He
made them comfortable, furnished the father
employment, and gave thanks to God that his
fellow - creatures were not suffered to perish
within sight of his own door.

Partly to prevent the distraction of his mind
from the more systematic plans of beneficence
he had in hand, and partly to discriminate wisely
between imposition and worthy objects of charity, so as to assure the relief of real suffering,
he engaged an excellent lady of the Society of
Friends to visit for him and distribute alms to
the deserving. A volume could be filled with
her recollections of his generosity.

THE GREAT FINANCIAL CRISIS.

THE locomotive works on Broad Street had been erected at a time of great apparent prosperity in the financial community. Money could be had on reasonable terms; universal confidence prevailed; prices were remunerative, and industry was greatly stimulated throughout the country. The new establishment began its career with the most flattering prospects. But very soon these sanguine expectations were disappointed. The immense investments and the future enterprise of the business seemed to be lost beyond recovery. To enable the present generation to understand the causes of this disaster, and to appreciate Mr. Baldwin's character when subjected to this trial, a brief retrospect will be necessary.

In the early part of 1832, the bill to recharter the United States Bank was vetoed by President Jackson. The merits of the question were fairly tried before the people at the Presidential election in the fall, and the President was sus-

tained and re-elected for a second term.   Sept.
18th, 1833, he laid before his cabinet the decision at which he had arrived, and in which the
people had sustained him, as he believed, to remove the public deposits from this Bank.   "It
is not easy for one who was not a living witness
of the fact, to realize the anxiety and alarm
which this threat excited in Philadelphia.   It
was known to all that the average amount of
these deposits, always considerable, had contributed to the Bank's loans and accommodations
in proportion to its amount, no less than its
capital; and that if the Bank was suddenly called
upon to return this money to the Government,
it must at once require repayment of much
which it had previously lent.   This must com-
pel forced sales of property at reduced prices,
ruinous rates of interest, and all the mischiefs
of a deficient circulation.   These evils, indu-
bitably great, were naturally exaggerated until
the whole mercantile community, and all who
sympathized with them, without distinction of
party, were thrown into as great a panic as sudden pecuniary distress could produce."*   The
most excited public meetings ever held in the

* Tucker's Hist. U. S., iv. 156.

city now assembled to denounce the measure. Two Secretaries of the Treasury surrendered their office rather than carry out the will of the President; so that the actual removal of the deposits from Philadelphia, and their distribution among the State Banks of the country, did not take place till November, 1833. The Bank immediately demanded the balances due it from the State banks, refused discounts to individuals, and called for repayments, total or partial, from all who had been formerly accommodated.

The distress in all the commercial towns from the scarcity of money continued throughout this and the following year. But early in 1835, the Bank of the United States and its branches, finding themselves in an easy condition in consequence of the large importations of specie which it had been the policy of the Government to encourage, by way of making bank paper less necessary, their accommodations were proportionally large; and thus the measures taken to lessen the amount of bank paper in circulation, served actually to increase it. Money being thus abundant, a spirit of speculation began to make its appearance in the larger cities, and went on increasing in them until it extended to the smaller towns, and finally to every part of the country. The minds of the people seemed to be in a state of intoxication from greediness of gain. This extravagance continued to grow until the following year, the local banks in every part of the country expanding their issues so as to keep the money market easy, until the prices of all articles of manufacture and importation were enormously increased. The tide began to turn in 1836, when the prices thus artificially raised by borrowed capital began to fall yet more suddenly than they had ever risen, and thousands who had indulged in dreams of ideal wealth encountered disappointment and ruin.*

The cause of this sudden and unexpected check to bank issues and bank credits, and the consequent scarcity of money, was generally attributed to a circular from the Treasury Department prohibiting land offices from receiving anything but specie in payment for public lands after August, 1836.† In a few months the gold and silver seemed to be flowing to the West, from the commercial centres of trade. Early in April, 1837, the difficulties had augmented

* Tucker's United States, iv. 230   † Idem, 269.

in every city of the Union, and in New York
there were strong indications that a crisis was at
hand; and by the close of May every bank in
the United States south of Boston, whatever
was its character or resources, had stopped payment.

That this circular was the immediate occasion
of the distress is undoubtedly true. But it must
have occurred, though somewhat later, as a
legitimate result of the excessive issues of the
banks; of their increased means of lending
based upon the deposits of the Government and
the influx of specie induced by Jackson; of the
wild spirit of speculation which had thereupon
ensued; and of the corresponding increase in
the expensiveness of living and of the consump-
tion of foreign luxuries.

It would have been idle, of course, for Mr.
Baldwin to attempt to meet his liabilities at
such a time. The suspension of specie payments by the Philadelphia banks on the 11th of
May was followed by the failure of a number
of the most responsible firms in the city. Consternation prevailed everywhere. The orders
which had been received at the works were
countermanded; payments were stopped on

work which had been sent out; the most dis-
heartening letters came pouring in from debtors
in every part of the country. In a short time
he was absolutely helpless.

He called a meeting of his creditors as soon
as he ascertained that suspension was inevitable.
They came together in alarm and suspicion,
each bringing his legal adviser, as was then the
custom. What was their amazement to see
Mr. Baldwin enter the room with a young clerk
bringing the papers from the office. He laid
before them, in the most lucid manner, an exact
statement of his assets and liabilities. He neither concealed nor exaggerated. With valuations
as they stood before the crash, he proved that
he could make them good. At present, he
candidly admitted that a forced sale would not
pay them twenty-five cents on the dollar.
"But the property belongs to you," he added.
"My factory and my house, and everything in
them and about them are yours. I release to
you, and, if you desire, will make over to you
at once, everything I possess on earth. Make
an inventory of all my effects, consider them
yours; then make up your mind what you will
do with them. If you cannot come to a satis-

factory conclusion, I have something to propose for our mutual advantage."

What could the lawyers do with such a man? They were prepared for subterfuge; but such straight-forward talk took away their occupation. The creditors began to think they might have left their legal gentlemen at home. The inventory was speedily made. Nothing was kept back. All the family treasures were brought out of their cherished retreats to have the auctioneer's price set upon them. It was a sad time in the Tenth Street house. But they were all sustained by the spirit of stern integrity which animated the principal sufferer. When the work, with all its harrowing details, was completed, the results were found to be as he had predicted. A peremptory sale would ruin him, and pay them a pittance of their just claims.

"Now," said he, "you are prepared for my proposition: Let me go on with the business, and I will pay you every dollar, with interest, in three years! I don't ask for an abatement of one cent. Give me an extension of three years, and you shall be fully reimbursed. I have no right to do this without your consent, for the property is yours. But say the word, and if my life is spared, every paper you hold against me shall be redeemed."

They took him at his word. Then came such a struggle as few men have been called upon to endure. The gravest difficulty was one which appealed to his feeling of humanity; the want of ready money to pay his workmen. He could obtain acceptances of his note for materials; but money could not be had in the market. He was obliged to resort to the expedient which had already begun to flood the city with private and depreciated currency. A few days after the suspension, the "blue ink" notes of twenty-five and fifty cents began to be issued. "Loan Companies," many of them voluntary and unchartered, were printing and distributing promises to pay in sums as low as six and a quarter cents. Private companies were obliged to make the same shifts. Mr. Baldwin would not consent to imitate the measures which in too many instances were fraudulent. He arranged with dealers in provisions, coal, and the most necessary articles of domestic life, to receive small orders from his office, and take his note for the sum when it had accumulated. For a long time these orders formed the only money his men could use. But he animated them all with his own confidence. When they saw that he asked no sacrifice of them which his own family did not cheerfully share, they endured their privations with an alacrity, and worked with an energy which was perfectly inspiring. Some of those who had saved their earnings in the "poor man's bank," the old cupboard at home, were able to let their wages accumulate now, and receive his note for large sums. Few of them ever tried to dispose of this paper. They had confidence that it would be as good as gold in time. One old man, now in the establishment, remembers this to his cost. He had let his earnings accumulate until he found himself holding Mr. Baldwin's notes to the amount of four hundred dollars. He happened to want the money when it could not be had at head-quarters, and nobody would buy it without a shave of some twenty per cent. At last he was foolish enough to invest in a land speculation. He lost every cent of it, and had the chagrin into the bargain to see it paid at the counter afterwards, with full interest.

The success of these manly endeavors was surprising. And a gradual relief to the finan-

cial pressure came to his assistance more speedily
than could have been expected. In August,
1838, many of the banks resumed payment, and
Mr. Baldwin began to call in some of the claims
against him. But one constitutional defect in
his character had betrayed him into imprudence
in this difficulty. He was always too fond of a
favorite idea, and so eager to realize it that his
determination verged upon obstinacy. He had
hastily promised to pay all in three years, and
toward the close of the specified period he began to cripple his business to fulfil the letter of
his engagement. Another disaster in the financial world added to his embarrassments. The
resumption of specie payments by the city banks
was found to be premature, as many of them
had feared, and another suspension followed in
October, 1839, occasioned by the sudden failure
of the Bank of the United States. With great
reluctance, and with a humiliation which he
bitterly felt, he was obliged to acknowledge
himself in difficulty again, and ask for another
extension. It was readily granted, and by 1841
or '2 he cancelled every obligation. It was a
magnificent triumph!

It was probably in one of these embarrassments that a capitalist in New Jersey offered him money on condition that a son of his should be received as a partner. He agreed, and for a time all went prosperously; but before long his difficulties were as great as ever. His partner's father sent for him, and proposed that a judgment should be confessed by the firm in his favor, under which a sheriff's sale would take place, and he become the purchaser. Mr. Baldwin rose in great indignation, and exclaimed:—

"Mr. ——, if this is all you have to say to me, you might have saved your breath. You shall never have the slightest advantage over my smallest creditor on account of your connection with the firm!"

It would be an indignity offered to the memory of this noble man, to claim that all this was anything more than strict honesty. But there have been times when honesty was more heroic than magnanimity would be now. The crisis of 1837 was one of those times. The most honorable merchants, and even presidents of the banks, were repeatedly indicted for embezzlements. In fact the grand jury were publicly charged with sitting as a secret inquisition, and bringing in indictments against the best citizens, without any previous examination. The consternation was so universal that men of untarnished reputation ceased to be surprised to find themselves accused of crime. Neighbors used to meet one another on the street, and actually burst into tears, exclaiming: "How hard it is to be an honest man in these times!"

How was he enabled to achieve such a triumph in those straitened times? By diligence, by the fascination of his courage animating all his associates, by carrying those burdens of his business always to the Throne of Grace, and receiving there a refreshment of spirit which filled the darkest day with the repose of unfaltering faith in God, and, above all, by another principle of his religion—by never arresting his charities during his financial embarrassments. Would to God that every Christian man of business could feel the force of his example in this respect! He believed that his charities in times of difficulty were his best investments. Notes for thousands of dollars had been repeatedly given away, when he had no money for donations. "Shall we trust God for our affairs, and not for His own?" he would ask, when charged with imprudence. "How can I expect life and prosperity to meet my present liabilities, if I handle this immense capital, and suffer none of its income to flow into the Lord's treasury?"

"How rich he would have been if he had not given so much away!" you will hear on every man's lips.   False!   He might have died in poverty!   It was his liberality united with his unwearied enterprise which secured his fortune. The testimony of God, which he always preferred to the wisdom of the world, is vindicated in this return to his bosom of the good measure, pressed down, shaken together, and running over.

THE CONVENTION OF 1837-8, AND THE ANTI-SLAVERY EXCITEMENT.

WHILE thus perplexed with his own financial embarrassments, Mr. Baldwin was called to new duties in the service of his country. He was elected to the Convention called to meet in Harrisburg on May 2d, 1837, to amend the State Constitution. He tried in vain to decline this honor. His financial troubles, the contract to furnish the engines for the ice boat, and his yet incomplete experiments with the locomotives for heavy draft, rendered his personal attention to business imperative, in his own opinion. But his fellow-citizens felt they could not dispense with his practical wisdom, and firm adherence to principle, on this important occasion. With great reluctance he laid aside his own interests to sit among the councillors of the commonwealth.

The two great questions which engaged the attention of this Convention concerned the judiciary and the right of suffrage.

By the Constitution of 1790 the judges of the Supreme Court and of the several Courts of Common Pleas were appointed by the Governor, and held their office during good behavior, subject to removal for any reasonable cause, on the address of two-thirds of each branch of the legislature. A so-called "reform" was introduced by this Convention, providing that these judges should be appointed by the Governor, by and with the advice of the Senate, and should hold their office for limited terms, not exceeding fifteen years in the case of the judges of the Supreme Court.*

This supposed reform prepared the way for more radical changes in 1850, by which the judges of the Supreme Court were elected by the qualified electors of the commonwealth at large, and all other judges by electors of the respective districts over which they were to preside or act as judges.†

A large majority of the Convention favored the proposed changes. But there was a determined minority, who steadily resisted these en-

---

* Proceedings and Debates of the Convention, XIII. 241.
† Purdon's Digest, p. 18.

croachments on what they believed to be the integrity of the judiciary. We find Mr. Baldwin's name always with these conservatives. He voted against every amendment to the fifth article of the old Constitution.*

The other question has since acquired a national importance, and is destined to rise above every other in the politics of the country; but it is one surrounded with the gravest difficulties, which have thus far baffled many of the most eminent statesmen of this nation and of England. Shall there be any limit to the exercise of the right of suffrage in a free government? If so, shall this limit be based upon property, or intelligence, or both? And is this a question of political privileges exclusively, or do moral principles enter into it founded upon the natural rights of man? These are among the momentous problems of modern reform agitating every constitutional government on earth. We shall be interested to know how they were met thirty years ago by an intelligent mechanic, without legal erudition, but with a conscience impervious to error and acutely sensitive to the truth.

* XIII. 48.

The Constitution of 1790 provided that:—
"Every freeman of the age of twenty-one years,
having resided in the State two years next before
an election, and within that time paid a State or
county tax, shall enjoy the right of an elector."*

The first motion to modify this article was
made by Mr. Steriger, of Montgomery County,
June 19th, 1837. He proposed to substitute for
"freeman" the words "free male *white* citizen."†
Finding that this was about to provoke a discussion too violent for this early period in the session, the friends of the amendment suffered the
debate to be diverted to other subjects. But Mr.
Martin, of Philadelphia, a few days later, endeavored to secure the same principle by means
of the following proviso: "Provided that the
rights of electors shall in no case extend to
others than free *white* male citizens."‡ In the
course of the debate upon this amendment the
assertion was repeatedly made that negroes never
did vote under the old constitution, "public
opinion rising above law, and driving them from
the polls with violence." But this statement
was met with the most conclusive evidence that

---

* Art. iii., Sec. 1st.   † Vol. ii. 472.   ‡ Vol. iii. 82.

in many parts of the State the franchise was peacefully exercised by colored men, some of them among the most intelligent and wealthy citizens of their districts. But all modifications of this nature were finally excluded from the report of the Committee of the Whole, not so much on the merits of the question as from the desire to avoid, at this early day, the agitation of the subject.

The question came up for final decision, Jan. 17th, 1838, when the second reading of the Third Article, as reported by the Committee of the Whole, was ordered; Mr. Martin again moved the insertion of the word "white" before "freeman."

The debate which ensued was continued incessantly and with great excitement, covering the whole question of American slavery, the proscription of a race, and the rights of manhood, until the vote was reached, on Saturday, January 20th. The amendment was sustained by a vote of 77 to 45. Among the forty-five men who had the courage and the conscience to vote for impartial suffrage, thirty years ago, we find M. W. Baldwin.*

* X. 106.

One more attempt was made to save the State from this disgrace. It was an amendment by Mr. Dunlap, of Franklin, to the effect that "any citizen excluded by the word 'white' may acquire the right of suffrage whenever he shall be possessed of a freehold worth two hundred dollars, and shall have paid a tax on the same; and that no male person of full age, not entitled to the rights of suffrage, shall be subject to direct taxation."* It was urged that a property qualification of this kind would protect the State from the dangers which had been described of vagrant and idle negroes controlling the elections; and the injustice of taxation without representation was forcibly represented. But this amendment was lost by a vote of 40 to 84, Mr. Baldwin voting in the affirmative.

Once more the effort was made, on motion of Mr. Merrill, of Union, to grant the right of suffrage to free citizens of color "who could read and understand common books, and were also subject to taxation."† It was insisted that both property and intelligence were safeguards which could not fail to protect this right from abuse. A final appeal was made to save the Keystone

* X. 110.   † X. 126.

State from this grave injustice. But in vain. At every vote the friends of impartial justice were falling away. This amendment was lost, 26 to 91, Mr. Baldwin still voting in the affirmative.

On the final question to agree to the report of the Committee of the Whole, which was reached January 22, 1838, Mr. Baldwin voted in the negative. Thus, during the whole of this exciting question, occupying the minds of the Convention during many days of a protracted session, his votes were invariably with that unpopular, conservative party, who believed that all men were born free and equal. Yet he lived to be denounced as a radical for holding the same views!

It was conscience, and religious principle, and faith in God, which sustained him in this struggle. His closet, the family altar, and his pastor's study, witnessed the fervor of his prayer for Divine guidance as the day of trial approached.

The friends of Mr. Baldwin will not need to be told that he was not a talking member of this Convention. While his own convictions of duty were decided, he had no confidence in his ability to make them felt by public speech. He threw the whole weight of his influence in favor of preserving the integrity of the laws, and the impartial rights of manhood. But it was by personal conversation, and consistent voting, that he made this influence felt. During the two protracted sessions of the Convention, he rose to his feet but once in the public debate. It was at the first meeting after the removal from Harrisburg to Philadelphia, on Tuesday, November 28th, 1837. The question before the house was a resolution of Mr. Denny, of Alleghany, that "the clergy of the city be invited to open the sessions of the Convention with prayer." Considerable opposition was at once developed. Many who were in favor of religious exercises, among others, Thaddeus Stevens, who "thought prayer very much needed," objected on the ground that members had been reluctant to pay any remuneration for similar services in Harrisburg.

The debate soon turned upon the question of compensation, when Mr. Baldwin took the floor. He said he felt authorized to say that the gentlemen who tendered their services here did not expect to receive any compensation. Indeed, he believed it was the intention of those gentlemen to disclaim compensation if it was tendered to them. He did not believe they would receive it.

He hoped, therefore, that this consideration would not be thrown in the way as an obstacle against the proposition to open the session with prayer. He must confess that he felt some surprise at the fears which had been expressed by some gentlemen, in relation to the conscientious scruples of certain members of this body on religious matters; for, when the question of conscientious scruples was fairly before them in another and not less imposing form, some of them did not manifest quite so sensitive a disposition. All that was contemplated by this resolution was, that we might each morning ask the blessing of Almighty God on the labors of the Convention. He could not conceive what reasonable objection could be made to this proposition by any gentleman, however sensitive might be his feelings, or however peculiar the religious doctrines which he held.*

These few remarks were subsequently referred to by almost every gentleman on the floor, and the motion was carried in the affirmative. The allusion to the "conscientious scruples" of men who had not hesitated to disfranchise their fellow-citizens on account of the color of their

---

* Proceedings and Debates of Convention, vi. 7.

skin was, perhaps, the nearest approach to sar-
casm which Mr. Baldwin ever made on any
public occasion.

It will be impossible to appreciate the courage
of Mr. Baldwin, and the "conservative" minority
with whom he voted, without reference to the
then existing state of public opinion which rendered their action so unpopular. The whole
country was in abject submission to the slave
power. The expression of anti-slavery sentiments was everywhere suppressed by violence.
"The right of free discussion," wrote John
Quincy Adams,* "upon slavery, and an indefinite
extent of topics connected with it, is banished
from one-half the States of this Union. It is
suspended in both houses of Congress—opened
and closed at the pleasure of the slave represen-
tatives; opened for the promulgation of nullification sophistry; closed against the question
WHAT IS SLAVERY? at the sound of which
the walls of the capitol stagger like a drunken
man. For this suppression of the freedom of
speech, the freedom of the press, and of the
right of petition, the people of the FREE States
are responsible, and the people of Pennsylvania

* History of Pennsylvania Hall, Phila., 1838, p. 11.

most of all. Of this responsibility, I say it with a pang sharper than language can express, the City of Philadelphia must take to herself the largest share. Her citizens have grown exceedingly averse to hearing any comment upon the self-evident truths which emanated from her Independence Hall. If a man makes any practical use of his freedom of speech among them, they cry out, 'He's a fanatic, an incendiary, an abolitionist; he is attacking the rights of the South.'"

A single example will set forth the extent to which this pro-slavery violence was carried in Philadelphia. The occasion which called forth this indignant letter of Adams' was the dedication of an imposing edifice erected on the corner of "Delaware Sixth and Haines Streets," for free discussion upon Liberty and the Rights of Man. The opening exercises were continued for several days, and the tone of the meeting soon gave unmistakable evidence that free speech in this city was too great a luxury not to be highly relished.

By evening of the second day large crowds had begun to collect around the building, and a few stones were thrown at the windows. The morning of the third day was devoted to free discussion on *Slavery and its Remedies*. The excitement was intense, but upon the announcement that several ladies would make addresses in the evening, the evidences of an approaching tumult became unmistakable. The hall was thronged long before the hour for the exercises to begin. Volleys of stones were thrown against the windows, and disorganizers within made repeated efforts to frighten the audience. Meantime placards had been posted all over the city, calling upon *all citizens who desired to preserve the Constitution of the United States to interfere forcibly and demand the immediate dispersion of the Convention.* The evidence was afterwards collected, which proved beyond doubt that the destruction of the hall had been resolved upon, before it was completed. The disturbances on Wednesday evening had been so violent that, on Thursday morning, the managers informed the Mayor that they anticipated the attacks of a mob, and demanded his protection of life and property; at the same time, in accordance with their well-known principles as Friends, they resolved to make no resistance, if violence should be offered. The Mayor made no reply to their communication, and left the hall to the incendiaries during the whole day,

without taking any measures to preserve order.
About sunset he informed the President of the
Board of Managers that he would disperse the
mob, if he could have possession of the building.
The keys were at once delivered to him. He
then addressed the mob, informing them that
there would be no meeting there on that evening,
that the military would not be called out, that
he relied upon his fellow-citizens now before
him as his police, and requested them to abide
by the laws and keep order. The mob then gave
three cheers for John Swift, the Mayor, and commenced the attack. They forced open the doors,
and, carrying papers and window blinds forward,
made a bonfire on the Speaker's stand. In a few
hours the magnificent building was entirely consumed. It was estimated that 15,000 spectators
witnessed this scene. The firemen were busy
protecting neighboring buildings. But no hand
was raised to save the Hall.* The unresisted
and infuriated mob then set fire to an orphan
asylum for colored children, on Thirteenth
Street, a charitable institution, having no connection with the Anti-Slavery Society; and, on
Saturday evening, attacked the Bethel Church

* Tucker's History of the U. S., iv. 336.

for colored people, on Sixth Street, and threatened the private dwellings of several citizens, and the office of the Public Ledger, which, though not an abolition paper, had been an advocate of free discussion, and had expressed itself in manly terms of disapprobation of the burning of the hall.

This was the time, be it remembered, when Mr. Baldwin voted incessantly for negro suffrage, in the city of Philadelphia. "Public opinion," said Mayor Swift, "makes mobs. Ninety-nine citizens out of a hundred, in Philadelphia, are against the abolitionists." Our war has since reversed this public opinion: ninety-nine out of a hundred have become abolitionists. But many of the best of these men still believe it to be imprudent to urge the impartial exercise of the right of suffrage. But, in Philadelphia, at the very time when the prejudice 'against the negro restrained the citizens and the civil authorities from interfering to prevent a most flagrant outrage upon public order, when threats of violence were openly made to intimidate the Convention, when he was ostracized by reason of these principles from the best society of the city his enterprise was enriching, when his name was sent

13

South in "black lists," designed to divert his profitable trade in that section to rival establishments, and when the mob were threatening the property of every abolitionist with the incendiary's torch, Mr. Baldwin stood unmoved to defend the right of the colored citizen, duly qualified, to the elective franchise!

LOCOMOTIVES FOR HEAVY FREIGHT, SHARP CURVES, AND ASCENDING GRADES.

IT would be natural to suppose that, while such exciting questions were enlisting so much of his attention, and while he was struggling to pay his oppressive debts, he would confine his manufacturing labors to the inventions which had already proved to be serviceable and remunerative. But the fact is precisely the reverse. During these years of perplexity and disaster, from 1837 to 1842, he was carrying on the most hazardous experiments of his whole career; and it was his inventive genius which finally rescued him from financial embarrassment. He at last perfected improvements in locomotives which not only increased immensely their power, but laid the foundation of his own fortune.

One of the gravest difficulties in the construction of locomotives for the transportation of heavy freight trains, is to secure sufficient adhesion to the track to prevent the driving

wheels from slipping. This difficulty was ima-
gined at first to be insurmountable by a smooth
driving wheel. Hence Trevethick's first engine
was constructed with wheels, the periphery of
which was made rough by the projection of bolts
or cross-grooves, so that their "grip" or "bite"
to the track might be secured. The jolts which
resulted from their rapid motion over the cast-
iron plates of the Merthyr-Tydvil road were
among the principal causes of Trevethick's failure. The next attempt to secure adhesion
was made by Mr. Blenkinsop, of Leeds, in
1811, who laid a racked or toothed rail on one
side of the road, into which a toothed driving
wheel on his locomotive worked, as pinions
work into a rack.* One year later, the Messrs.
Chapman, of Newcastle, endeavored to overcome
the same fictitious difficulty by passing a chain
once round a grooved barrel-wheel under the
centre of the engine, so that when the wheel
turned, the locomotive, as it were, dragged itself
along the railway by means of this immense
chain, stretching for miles along the track.
These grotesque experiments were not abandoned until, in 1813, Mr. Brusston, of Derby-

* Annals of Leeds, vol. II. p. 222.

shire, mounted a steam engine on legs, working alternately like those of a horse, which fortunately blew up at one of its first trials, killed only a few of the bystanders, and prevented worse mischief for the future.

In 1813 an experiment was tried to secure adhesion to the smooth rail, by Mr. Wm. Hedley, of Wylam. His first engine constructed on this principle was a perfect success, and has been at work, near Newcastle, as late as 1863. Mr. Stephenson relied upon the weight of his engines to secure adhesion up to the maximum of their power. It was thus supposed that this early difficulty was purely fictitious.

But the perfection of Mr. Baldwin's ground joints for steam pipes, the substitution of wire for hemp and other fibrous materials in packing, the increased size of his boilers, together with the admirable finish of all the parts, gave a tremendous power to his engines, and enabled them to surpass the maximum of adhesion which their immense weight imparted. There was also a limit to the weight which could be thrown upon two, or even four driving wheels. The rails might be crushed by receiving nearly the whole weight of the machine upon a limited section.

The problem was to distribute the weight over all the wheels, fore and aft, and yet make them all draw. This occasioned no difficulty so long as the road was straight, as the wheels could be made of a uniform size, and simply coupled. Six or eight wheel locomotives were manufactured by Mr. Stephenson, and succeeded in rounding curves of large radius by having flanges only on the four external wheels. But the wheels without flanges were almost wrenched from the track in rounding the curves, losing much of their adhesion when it was most needed, and endangering the machinery. Besides, the very roads which transported the heaviest freights of coal, and encountered the worst ascending grades, were also obliged to turn the shortest curves.

Mr. Baldwin's struggle with these difficulties brought out some of the grandest traits of his character. He seemed to grasp all the conditions of the problem at once, and yet to concentrate his thoughts as if but one obstacle were in his way. Strange as it may seem, also, the state of his health, which would have defeated all exertion in many men, was made to assist him. He could not sleep, and he employed the night in busy invention. While his exhausted body was in an attitude of repose, he made the darkness luminous with imaginary "wheels within wheels."

The first result of these incessant contrivances was his six-wheeled gear locomotive, patented December 31, 1841. In this ingenious machine the four wheels of the truck were placed forward, in the usual way, and the pistons had outside connections with the two driving wheels behind the fire-box. The truck was permitted to vibrate freely, and accommodate itself to the curves and undulations of the road. The axles of the truck wheels were thus thrown incessantly into positions not parallel to the axle of the drivers. But between the two axles of the truck was placed a revolving shaft, held firmly in a position parallel to the driving axle, and at right-angles to the axis of the boiler, by stays connected with the frame of the locomotive. On the middle of this shaft, which was made to revolve by a crank and a rod connecting with the drivers, a cog-wheel was fixed, having chilled cogs, slightly rounded on the face, which, by means of two intervening wheels, gave motion to others on the axis of the truck. The four truck wheels were made of any desirable size, as the gearing was proportioned so as to make them travel at the rate of the larger wheels.* The results obtained by this engine, we learn from the Report of G. A. Nicholls, Superintendent of Transportation on the Philadelphia Reading and Pottsville R. R.:† a train of 117 loaded cars, weighing in the aggregate 590 tons, was hauled fifty-four miles in five hours and twenty-two minutes, being at the rate of over ten miles per hour the whole way. The train was more than a quarter of a mile in length, and was transported in the ordinary freight business, without any previous preparation of the engine, cars, or fuel, for the performance. The engine was closely watched at all the starts of the train, and not the least slipping of her wheels could be perceived. She worked remarkably well throughout the trip, turning curves of 819 feet radius, with ease to her machinery, and no perceptible increase of friction in her gearing. The engine afterwards backed with ease round a curve of 75 feet radius. This train was unprecedented in length and weight in Europe and America.

But so much power was lost by friction, and the danger of breaking and derangement was so

* Journal of Franklin Institute, March, 1842, p. 178.
† U. S. Gazette, Feb. 14, 1842.

great, in this complicated machinery, that Mr.
Baldwin regarded what others praised so highly,
as a practical failure. Without a disheartened
feeling for a single moment, he returned to his
absorbing studies. Every day he would bring
new contrivances to his draughtsmen, and take
home, at night, the difficulties which they encountered in the construction. He came back
at last to the Stephenson model of making all
the wheels of a uniform size, and uniting them
by connecting rods. The improvement which
he resolved to work out, was to avoid the rigidity
of this machine. The arrangement which at
last proved to be successful, occurred to him
suddenly in the depths of the night. He sprang
out of bed, made a few rough drawings, and
waited with burning impatience for the morning. On repairing to the works, he found the
Sheriff's bills of sale posted all over the premises,
and the men standing about in the greatest consternation. The financial crisis had occurred on
the very day of his greatest invention. He
stretched out his right hand, containing his roll
of rude drawings, and said in a tone of triumph:

"I have something here which will defy the
Sheriff."

14

Before leaving the office to propose the settlement with his creditors which we have already described, he placed his sketches, with full explanations, in the hands of the draughtsmen. They shared his ardor at first, and the enthusiasm of the inventor spread like a contagion among the dispirited workmen. But obstacles were encountered in the construction of the model, which discouraged all but himself. "It must work; it *shall* work," was his uncompromising reply to their objections. And after a delay of more than a year it did work. He produced a "Flexible Truck Locomotive," which was the best machine ever invented for the transportation of burdens on roads of heavy grades and short curvature.

It will be impossible to render a description of the details of this invention intelligible without illustrations. But its general principle can be readily comprehended. In a locomotive of two driving wheels, there are only two points of contact with the rail which must maintain a constant relative distance from the cylinders; because the truck forward is permitted to vibrate freely around the single pivot on which that part of the frame of the locomotive rests. But when

the three or four wheels on each side are bound
together by an inflexible connecting-rod, as in
the rigid engines, a crowding and slipping motion around the curves results, at a great loss of
power and peril of the machinery.   Mr. Baldwin's improvement consists in attaching the four
wheels forward to a flexible truck, instead of the
rigid frame of the locomotive.   In the ordinary
truck, the two axles with the lateral beams of
the frames form the figure of a rectangle.   The
flexible truck is so constructed that this figure
may be changed to a parallelogram of various
angles, like a parallel ruler.   The frame of the
locomotive rests upon two pivots instead of one,
inserted in the side beams of this truck.

The action of the locomotive in rounding a
curve will now be readily understood.   The
wheels are all of a uniform size, and are united
by connecting rods.   The pistons move the
driving-wheels in the rear in the usual way, and
they move the truck wheels forward.   So long
as the track is straight, the axles of all the wheels
maintain a position at right angles to the axis of
the boiler.   But as soon as the truck wheels encounter a curve, those on the inside track begin
to move in advance of the corresponding ones

on the outside. The frame of the truck is thus
changed from a rectangle to a parallelogram,
the angles of which continue to change round
the whole curve. To accommodate these varia-
tions, the following parts of the machine are
made flexible:—

First. The frame of the truck is constructed
with joints at the four angles, like those of the
parallel ruler.

Second. The wrought iron beams forming
the sides of this truck contain cylindrical boxes
in each end for the journal bearings of the axles.
These boxes vibrate readily in their sockets and
adapt themselves to the oblique motion of the
axles.

Third. In the frame of the locomotive two
spherical pins are fixed, as pivots, which rest in
sockets on the centres of the two lateral beams.
Each beam is thus allowed to vibrate on this
point; the spherical joint accommodating irregularities of elevation as well as curvature.

Fourth. The connecting rods have universal
joints at the points of contact with the wheels.
While the relative distance between each driving
wheel and its corresponding truck wheel at the
extreme front is thus constant, the several sec-

tions of the connecting rod are not held rigidly in a straight line.

To avoid the resistance of the tender, the water is carried in a tank placed on the boiler, and the fuel is stored in two boxes on each side of the foot-board, lengthened for this purpose. Thus the entire weight of the locomotive with its supplies, amounting in some instances to thirty tons, is economized to secure adhesion, the labor is impartially distributed among all the wheels, while all irregularities of the track are accommodated as readily as by locomotives of two driving wheels.

The patent for the Flexible Truck Locomotive was secured in August, 1842,* and its performances have since led to the construction of roads in this and other countries over heights before deemed inaccessible. Mr. Charles Ellet, Jr., in his description of the "Mountain Top Track" across the Blue Ridge in Virginia, which exceeded in difficulty of construction the famous Austrian Road over the Lemmercing Pass, does not hesitate to ascribe to this locomotive in climbing steep grades, unrivalled pre-eminence.

* Journal of Franklin Institute, August, 1848, p. 93.

The maximum grade on this road is 296 feet per mile, and it has curvatures of 234 feet radius. He says:—

"This road was opened to the public in the spring of 1854, and it has now, in the autumn of 1856, been in constant use for a period of more than 2½ years. In all that time the admirable engines relied on to perform the extraordinary duties imposed upon them in the passage of this summit, have failed *but once* to make their regular trips. The mountain has been covered with deep snows for weeks in succession, and the cuts have been frequently filled for long periods many feet in depth with drifted snow; the ground has been covered with sleet and ice, and every impediment due to bad weather and inclement seasons has been encountered and successfully surmounted in working the track.

"During the last severe winter, when the travel upon all the railways of Virginia and the northern and western States was interrupted, and, on many lines, for days in succession, the engines upon this mountain track, with the exception of the single day already specified, moved regularly forward and did their appointed work. In fact, during the space of 2½ years that the road has been in use, they have only failed to take the mail through in this single instance, when the train was caught in a snow-drift near the summit of the mountain.

"These results are due, in a great degree, to the admirable adaptation of the engines employed to the service to be performed. The regular daily service of each of the engines is to make four trips of eight miles over the mountain, drawing one eight-wheel baggage car together with two eight-wheel passenger cars, in each direction.

"In conveying freight, the regular train on the mountain is three of the eight-wheel house cars fully loaded, or four of them when empty or partly loaded.

"These three cars, when full, weigh with their loads from 40 to 43 tons. Sometimes, though rarely, when the business has been unusually heavy, the loads have exceeded 50 tons.

"With such trains the engines are stopped on the track, ascending or descending, and are started again, on the steepest grades, at the discretion of the engineer.

"The ordinary speed of the engines, when loaded, is $7\frac{1}{2}$ miles an hour on the ascending grades, and from 5½ to 6 miles an hour on the descent.

"Greater speed and larger loads might doubtless be permitted with success; but the policy has been to work the track with perfect safety, to risk nothing, and to obtain and hold the public confidence.

"The locomotives mainly relied on for this severe duty were designed and constructed by the firm of M. W. Baldwin & Company, of Philadelphia. The slight modifications introduced at the instance of the writer to adapt them better to the particular service to be performed in crossing the Blue Ridge, did not touch the working proportions or principle of the engines, the merits of which are due to the patentee, M. W. Baldwin, Esq."

This magnificent locomotive continues to be without a rival in its peculiar and most difficult field. It is hurrying the produce of the West over the precipitous Alleghanies, scaling the mountain heights of Brazil, and flying with the wings of the morning across the western prairies, impatient for hardy enterprise to open the way for new triumphs over those rocky and snow-crested barriers which have too long severed us from the golden plains on the Pacific; animated, as it were, in all these incredible conquests of nature, with the determined spirit and unfaltering faith of its great inventor.

We cannot close this sketch of Mr. Baldwin's mechanical career without again calling attention to those sterling elements of his character which it has brought into exercise: his high genius, his ready adaptation to new pursuits, his buoyant hope and unfaltering faith in the midst of discouragement, his persistence in untried fields of labor, his inexhaustible patience in a chosen purpose, and, above all, his wise foresight have enabled him always to lead public enterprise in this country, made him prominent in every occupation he has undertaken, and constituted him a public benefactor merely by the new industry he has stimulated, and the encouraging example he has set before every young man who engages in honorable labor with high aspirations.

CHURCH BUILDING.

Long after Mr. Baldwin's fame as a locomotive builder shall have been consigned to the comparative oblivion of technical history, his name will be remembered with gratitude by thousands. He was emphatically the church builder of Philadelphia.

This work began little by little in the Missionary Association. Their Mission Sabbath Schools would bring families within the means of grace who never entered a Christian church. Prayer meetings and informal addresses on the Sabbath would call for more permanent labors. A minister of the gospel would be engaged and a congregation gathered; then a church would be provided. The Western Presbyterian Church, corner of Seventeenth and Filbert Streets, grew out of the labors of this Association, and the first large contribution Mr. Baldwin ever made in this favorite work of beneficence was to save the Cedar Street Presbyterian Church from sheriff's sale.

CALVARY CHURCH.

But the beginning of this great work of Church extension will always be dated from a more important enterprise. In the fall of 1850 Mr. Barnes met Mr. Baldwin and another member of his church, at one of his pastoral visits, and the conversation turning upon the migration of families west of Broad Street, they decided to call a meeting to consider the needs of this growing neighborhood. Dr. Brainard soon entered into the plan with his accustomed zeal. The meetings continued to adjourn from week to week, until more than a dozen of the most substantial and earnest Christian men from the congregations of the First, Pine Street, and Clinton Street churches were interested in the deliberations. Forty successive meetings in all were held. They were of one mind, but, unfortunately, the subscriptions could not be brought up to anything like the required sum. At last Dr. Brainard made one of his characteristic speeches. Only a month or two before his death he happened to relate the circumstance to a friend, so that this little model of persuasive

eloquence can be preserved almost in his exact
words: "I made up my mind," said he, "that
Brother Barnes and I were dealing a little too
tenderly with our rich friends.   I was not afraid
of them, and thinking the time had now come
for pretty plain talk, I said to them :—

"Brethren, the Lord has denied to you the
privilege of exercising many of the most precious graces of the Christian character, which
in his infinite mercy he has vouchsafed to the
rest of us. You never knew what it is to repose
absolute unassisted faith in God for the things
of this world. You never had to go to sleep at
night without knowing where your breakfast
was to come from. You never had a sick child
wasting away for want of costly luxuries. You
never had to deny yourselves the gratification of
the impulses of pity when a sufferer came to
your door. You never had to endure the humiliation of being dunned for an honest debt
without knowing whether you could ever pay it.
All these unspeakable advantages in developing
Christian character an inscrutable Providence
has taken from you and bestowed upon us poor
men. The one solitary grace of the Christian
life which has been denied to us and given to

you, is the grace of liberality, *and if you don't exercise that, the Lord have mercy on your souls!*"

Every one who ever heard Dr. Brainard talk when he meant it, can see the upturned face, sparkling eye, and compressed lip with which these pungent words came out. As he reached this part of the narrative to his friend on that memorable ride in the summer of 1866, he reined in his horse and broke out in the heartiest tone: "My confidence in human nature was not misplaced. At first I was almost frightened at my boldness; but soon I saw one of those amused and genial smiles begin to creep over Baldwin's face. Somebody caught the twinkle of his eye, and in half a minute the whole company broke into inextinguishable laughter. In two or three weeks we had some $75,000 on the paper."

Mr. Baldwin's portion of this subscription, $10,000, was the smallest part of his offering in the good work. He was indefatigable in his personal attention to the work of selecting the ground, drawing the plans, and securing the prompt execution of the contract. The corner stone was laid on the fourth day of July, 1851, and Nov. 6th, 1853, one of the most beautiful and imposing church edifices in the city was

dedicated to the service of Almighty God. Four
days later the church was organized, with Mr.
Baldwin and Mr. Thomas Fleming as ruling
Elders, and Mr. John A. Brown as President of
the Board of Trustees; all from the First Presbyterian Church.

It was the intention of Mr. Baldwin and some
of the largest contributors to this fund, that it
should be considered a *bona fide* offering to the
Lord, without any reserve of personal property
in the building; that no part of their subscriptions should ever be paid back from the sale of
pews, but that all moneys derived from this
source should constitute a perpetual fund for
erecting new churches in the city of Philadelphia as they were needed. It is impossible to
conceive a more magnificent plan of church
extension. Each church could be built with
cash payments, and could repay the advances
made in its own time of prosperity, thus enabling
others in turn to continue the good work. But
unfortunately this feature of the new enterprise
was not carried out, and the fund from the sale
of pews was distributed among the original sub-
scribers.

But although the plan failed, the spirit of

church extension was infused into the Calvary congregation from the beginning. The work was stimulated by the vigorous appeals of the Pastor. New Sabbath Schools and new congregations began to be gathered at once. The munificence of many members of this branch of the church began to be directed to this one means of doing good above all others. Foremost among these eager church builders was Mr. Baldwin.

OLIVET CHURCH.

The first enterprise* of this kind was a Sabbath School, organized in 1855, in the northwestern part of the city by a few members of Calvary Church. In a few weeks it overflowed the small premises at first provided.

In this extremity the Missionary Association of Calvary Church, who had pledged themselves to the support of the school, called upon the Pastor, Mr. Brown, and Mr. Baldwin, to visit the neighborhood and judge of the demands for enlargement. They took a grand survey of the

* This part of our narrative was kindly furnished by Rev. W. W. Taylor, Pastor of Olivet Church.

whole ground. They discussed the expediency of taking down partitions.and making the house then occupied serviceable. This was abandoned at once as inadequate. At last they ascended an eminence on the corner of Twenty-second and Mount Vernon Streets, whence at that day they could look eastward for half a mile over unoccupied ground, and every mind was at work thinking and planning. Evidently a new building must be erected. But the sum demanded would be large; and without a liberal offer to begin with, the Association would not dare to move.

Mr. Baldwin was one of the most remarkable men who ever lived, to foresee the demands of the future. The same spirit which anticipated the application of steam to railroads, grasped now, at one glance of the eye, the more urgent demands of this growing part of the city for gospel work. Throwing his hand in the direction of Spring Garden and Twenty-fourth Street, he exclaimed: "I have a lot over there worth six thousand dollars; you may have it."

The offer was so generous and unexpected that it was not at once appreciated, the brethren of the Association supposing he meant to let them build on it, subject to ground rent: thus the exploration was brought to a close with no definite results. Not long after he inquired, with considerable surprise, "What are you waiting for? Why don't you build on my lot?" producing a plot he had made of its situation and dimensions. Encouraged now with the assurance of this liberal gift out and out, they began to get plans for building, and, with Mr. Baldwin's cordial consent, disposed of the land to pay for the erection of the new chapel. Very soon the welcome intelligence was received that Mr. Brown had pledged an equal amount for the purchase of the place of good omen, where the survey of the ground had first been made. On a portion of this lot of 140 feet front on Twenty-second Street, occupying the whole block between Mount Vernon and Wallace Streets, with 100 feet depth, a beautiful and commodious chapel was built. Here the Sabbath School was gathered, and within a year a church with sixteen members and two ruling elders was organized, under the name of the Olivet Presbyterian Church.

In 1861 Rev. W. W. Taylor was called to this church, and under his efficient labors the

16

congregation again increased beyond its accommodations. Besides, buildings were going up all around the little chapel, which demanded that a more beautiful edifice should be reared to the honor of God's name. Again, therefore, the faithful Pastor and his people, rich in faith, but not yet in substance, applied to their generous friends. But this was in 1863; and the uncertainties of the great war operated against their claims on the mind of one of them, while the other had previously pledged all his available means to another church. No entreaty could induce Mr. Baldwin to make any pledges for the distant future. "One thing at a time," he would say to the good brethren, with such kindness that they did not despair.

Early in 1864 Mr. Taylor made another visit to that consecrated office where more business for the next world than for this was transacted. The works and gifts of this good man were conducted on principles of wise Christian calculation; nor was one word of argument or persuasion needed when he saw clearly the point of duty and wisdom. He had just paid the last bills of his recent engagement; but so far was he from feeling that his work was done and he might now rest from care, his hands had only grown fuller and his heart larger for new liberality.

He therefore asked for a frank and full statement of their necessities. Mr. Taylor had not proceeded far when he was interrupted with the welcome question:—

"Well, what kind of a church do you want?"

The reply was that $25,000 would furnish them with all that they needed, but a building less sightly and commodious than that sum would procure ought not to be erected.

"But where in the world do you expect to get that much money?"

"I don't know," was the reply, "unless you give it."

"And what reason have you to suppose that I will?"

"We have the impression that you have invested too much money in our work already to see your stock depreciate on your hands."

Mr. Baldwin loved nothing so much as outspoken frankness, without flattery or management. With a hearty smile he gave the hard working pastor his hand, and said:—

"Go ahead and select your model."

No firmer promise than these words implied was needed: that very day the delightful work of prospecting and planning was commenced, and on May 30th, 1864, the corner-stone of the present imposing edifice was laid. It was dedicated to the service of Almighty God on the last Sabbath of October, 1865, Mr. Baldwin's donation of $20,000 having been promptly paid.

And now another visit was made to the consecrated office. The Pastor and a committee of the Board of Trustees made a formal call to express their sense of obligation for his large generosity. Their sentiments and feelings were conveyed to him in simple words, entirely free from that fulsome eulogy which he could never endure. They seized upon the strong point which they knew he would appreciate, that they had needed his help, and that he had bestowed his substance wisely, where firm foundations had been laid for continuous good, and fountains of religious blessings opened that would continue to flow when many generations had passed away. They thanked him for his benefactions, and gave him their best wishes for his welfare, and the assurance of their prayers that God would reward him with grace and peace.

His reply to this affecting address was full of noble words, characteristic of his simple and devoted spirit: God had given him property to be used for his glory; it was nothing but his duty to give it away. He was moved and gratified by the testimony they gave him of their esteem; and he felt stimulated by what had passed to go on repeating what he had already done as long as God should spare his life. Thus ended their memorable interview with the good man who has gone before, whom they hope to meet where they who sow and they who reap shall rejoice together.

This narrative has been given here, although two other churches had been previously erected chiefly through Mr. Baldwin's munificence, because Olivet was the first daughter of Calvary. But she has a sister only two years younger, whose history is quite as intimately associated with Mr. Baldwin's life.

TABOR CHURCH.

On March 8th, 1857,[*] a Sunday School was opened under the direction of the Philadelphia Sunday School Association, in a small house on Monroe Street, between Seventeenth and Eighteenth. At that time it was estimated that more than thirty thousand children were destitute of religious instruction, and although there was a large population in this section, there was no Sunday School south of Lombard Street and west of Broad. This school, at its commencement, numbered twenty-three scholars and four teachers. The next Sunday, March 15th, classes were formed, and the school was called "Tabor." The next month the Missionary Association of Calvary Church, encouraged by the success which had crowned their efforts in the northern part of the city, which had resulted in the establishment of Olivet Church in a little over a year from the opening of the Mission Sunday School, took this school under its charge.

[*] From the Historical Sketch, prepared by Rev. Llewellyn Pratt, and read at the dedication of Tabor Church. See American Presbyterian, Dec. 22, 1864.

Anticipating its growth, the Association began at once to make arrangements to provide it with a suitable building. Before these could be perfected, however, the school had outgrown its two small rooms in Monroe Street, and was compelled, in May, to remove to larger ones at the corner of Seventeenth and Catharine Streets. Here, in a few weeks, the number of scholars increased to eighty-one.

At the close of July, 1857, a lot at the corner of Seventeenth and Fitzwater Streets having been given for that purpose by John A. Brown, Esq., ground was broken for the erection of a chapel 33 by 70 feet, and in about three months the building was completed at a cost, including the lot, of about seven thousand five hundred dollars. This neat and commodious chapel was dedicated on Nov. 16th, 1857, and the Sabbath School, numbering now one hundred and forty-five scholars, was removed to the first story, which alone was yet furnished. At once the growth was greatly stimulated, so that, before the end of the first year, three hundred and twenty-four scholars overflowed into the other story and took possession of the whole house. The school would never stay where it was put.

The Missionary Association could hardly keep pace with it, but was hurried on from one scheme of preparation to larger ones. It seemed as if those twenty-three scholars would become a host, all clamoring for room.

But the Association, under the lead of Mr. Pratt, its zealous Chairman, was not satisfied with the Sabbath School work. The chapel was soon opened for preaching on Sunday evenings, and for other religious services during the week, and it was at once proved that a congregation could be easily and speedily gathered, for the most part from those who had no regular place of worship. Provision was therefore made for the support of an Evangelist, who should preach regularly in the chapel and visit from house to house, for the spiritual good of the families in this neighborhood. By the good providence of God, the Association was led to procure the services of Rev. George Van Deurs, a native of Denmark, and a recent graduate of Auburn Seminary. He commenced preaching about the middle of July, 1858, and through his unwearied and faithful labors a large congregation was soon brought together, and the reforming work of the Holy Spirit was begun in this section of the city. The converts were at first received into Calvary Church, at its successive communions; but as their number increased the session of Calvary Church would meet at the Chapel to receive them, and also to celebrate the communion there.

Mr. Baldwin's interest in the enterprise began with Mr. Van Deurs' labors. It was his motion in the Association that an evangelist be employed; and as a "motion" from him was always more than a form of words, they had no fear that the funds would be raised. But the meetings of session in the Chapel secured an investment from him of more value than his generous donations—his heart was immediately interested in the spiritual good of these multitudes. Through wet and cold he would always find his way down to engage in the holy duties of his office to "try the spirits whether they be of Christ." Many of them had been brought up in great ignorance of religious truth, and spiritual doubts and troubles were often encountered. Nothing could exceed the tenderness with which this good man would lead these lambs of the fold. He never confused them with the perplexities of theology. He was not shocked to

17

find his questions answered very wildly sometimes. He knew the difference between faith
and opinion, and no soul who could say—

> "I'm a poor sinner, nothing at all;
> Jesus Christ is all in all,"

failed to receive his welcome and his blessing.
To the last day of their lives these little ones in
Jesus' fold will remember the first time they
received the bread and wine from this venerable
servant of the Lord.

There were thus admitted to this branch of
Calvary Church, from December, 1858, to April,
1863, two hundred and forty-three persons, all
but seven on confession of faith. These accessions were made regularly at every communion;
never less than three, in May, 1860, and in
February, 1861, thirty-five; an average on each
communion of thirteen. The time had now
come for the final stage in this important enterprise. On April 23d, 1863, a commission from
the Third Presbytery of Philadelphia, consisting
of Rev. Drs. Jenkins and Patton, Rev. George
Van Deurs, and Elder M. W. Baldwin, organized
the "Tabor Presbyterian Church in the City of
Philadelphia," with two hundred and thirteen
members, two ruling elders, and three deacons.

The influence of this step was at once felt, and soon Sabbath school and congregation were again clamoring for more room. The Association for once became alarmed at the irrepressible growth of their original twenty-three children. The clouds of war were dark over the land, and how could they make suitable provision for this vigorous church? We may imagine their relief to learn that the work of church building was for once taken out of their hands. Mr. Baldwin had often *helped* build churches; the time had come when he could build a church alone! Without waiting for one word of solicitation; without even consulting any one; in fact, against the remonstrance of some of his more cautious friends, he procured a large lot on the corner of Eighteenth and Christian Streets, and contracted for the erection of the church. July 2d, 1863, the corner-stone was laid by Miss Cecilia Baldwin, and appropriate addresses were made by Mr. Barnes, Dr. Brainard, Dr. March, and Mr. Culver. That day will be remembered by those who participated in the ceremonies as one of the dark days of the republic. It was the day before the battle of Gettysburg, when our own State was polluted by the touch of rebels; when rumors of disasters filled the air and made the heart sick; when hastening fugitives were coming to tell exaggerated and alarming tales of the near approach of the country's enemies. It will be remembered how difficult it was then to speak with hopefulness of the work undertaken; and doubt was even expressed whether the building thus commenced would soon be completed. This expression was on every one's tongue: but "the building of the walls of Jerusalem was ever in troublous times." With heavy hearts they deposited their relics in the stone, not the least precious of which was a striking portrait of the munificent builder of the proposed structure, and laid it to its long rest.

How changed the scene when, on the evening of Thursday, December 15th, 1864, this beautiful church was dedicated! The clouds had broken and drifted away. Though war was still raging in the land, this city had been undisturbed, and the building had reached completion without the slightest interruption. The style of Tabor Church is the early English, beautiful in design, harmonious in its proportions, and well adapted to all the purposes of public worship. It is on the cruciform or transept plan, with an elegant tower on one front angle, surmounted with a spire. The front measures 51.6

feet, the depth is 90.8; the transverse dimension through the transept is 78.6. The ceiling is a pointed arch, and decorated with moulded ribs. The height to the spring of the arch is 16 feet; to the apex 35 feet. It is built entirely of solid brown freestone, and is capable of seating 800 persons. The whole expense of $22,000 was paid by Mr. Baldwin.

The increase of this church has been such a remarkable illustration of the blessing of God upon this munificent gift, and upon faithful preaching, and the most indefatigable personal visitation by the pastor which any city has ever enjoyed, that we give a summary of the accessions to Tabor Church up to the present time:—

In 1859	. . 61	In 1865	. . 81
In 1860	. . 89	In 1866	. . 84
In 1861	. . 47	In 1867	. . 85
In 1862	. . 27		———
In 1863	. . 53	Total number 563	
In 1864	. . 36		

No wonder that Mr. Baldwin exclaimed, on the occasion of the anniversary of the Sabbath School in May, 1865, when for the first and last time he entered the new church, "This is the best investment I ever made in my life!"

NORTH BROAD STREET CHURCH.

Meantime another church enterprise had been originated by Mr. Baldwin, and had proved to be in many respects the most successful effort of the Presbyterian denomination in the city. Its history is a marvellous illustration of that wise foresight in spiritual matters which we have so often remarked.

In 1835, when the Broad Street works were erected, they were in the suburbs of the city; but the employment furnished by this and many similar enterprises which began to spring up on every side, stimulated the building of residences, until this outpost became the centre of the city. Mr. Baldwin had long been deliberating upon the best means of providing the Gospel for this field, so intimately associated with his severest struggles and greatest prosperity, when he made the acquaintance of Rev. E. E. Adams, who came to solicit contributions for the American Chapel in Paris.

One morning, in the spring of 1857, they met providentially on Chestnut Street.

"You are the very man I am looking for,"

said Mr. Baldwin, taking Mr. Adams' arm. "I am told that you are willing to undertake a new church enterprise in this city."

"Yes, sir," was the reply. "On certain conditions I would not object."

"And what are the conditions?"

"That it shall not be a *mission church*, nor a church for the rich exclusively; that all classes in the neighborhood shall be gathered in; and that my own support be pledged for two years, while I am doing the preliminary work of collecting a self-supporting congregation and erecting a house of worship."

"Very well; I thoroughly approve of your principles, and I desire to see them carried out in a new church near my factory. I will secure a hall, fit it up in an attractive way, pay your salary for two years, and give a lot on Broad Street for the church edifice."

The work began at once. The whole neighborhood was canvassed by the indefatigable pastor, and his genuine eloquence soon attracted a large congregation. Earnest workers were enlisted in the Sabbath school. Nearly every Presbyterian church in the city, and many others of kindred denominations, dismissed faithful mem-

bers to the new field. Their interest thus became enlisted in the new enterprise, and Mr.
Baldwin was soon sustained by the advice, encouragement, and sympathy of a large body of
Christian pastors. But advice always implies
the liberty of criticizing; and it was soon very
evident that his choice of a pastor was not entirely satisfactory to all. So long as he could
keep this quiet opposition from the knowledge
of the pastor, he gave it no attention. But he
soon found that it was exerting a depressing influence upon Mr. Adams, who, in fact, expressed
the determination to retire from the field. Nothing could exceed the bright and genial spirit
with which he endeavored to dispel this gather-
ing despondency.

"Come, now," said he at last, "you and I have
made one bargain, let us make another: you leave
these good brethren to me for six months; go
on with your work that long without a thought
of their antagonism; then if they do not sing
your praises as loud as any man, I will let you go."

His prediction was fulfilled. Perhaps the refreshment of such sympathy as this contributed
more than anything else to the elasticity of mind
and fervency of spirit in the new pastor which

soon secured universal approbation. A band of united Christian men soon gathered round him, with wealth, and liberality, and devotion to the good work; and the ground for the new building, on the corner of Broad and Green Streets, was soon broken. Meantime the outbreak of the Rebellion had created a panic in financial circles, and they began to fear that Mr. Baldwin's large subscription was in peril. A timid deputation called one day at the office, and made known their anxiety to one of the clerks.

"Is Mr. Baldwin's signature on your paper?" he asked.

They displayed the well-known autograph.

"Make your contracts, then, without hesitation. That promise is as good as gold here, whenever you choose to apply."

The solid stone edifice, beautiful in proportion and commanding in position, rose rapidly to completion. On its dedication it was filled by an intelligent congregation. And Mr. Baldwin lived to see this church attain a membership of 450, with Sabbath Schools of 400 members, and contributions to various benevolent objects amounting, in one year, to more than $50,000!

18

HERMON CHURCH.

It was a favorite idea with this good man to name the several churches which his munificence assisted to establish, after the sacred localities of the Bible. He proposed to give the name of "Carmel" to the North Broad Street Church, and failing to gain the consent of other contributors, afterwards suggested this name for the beautiful chapel on the corner of Broad and Oxford Streets, to which he contributed about eight thousand dollars. His last church edifice he named "Hermon." This he intended as a grateful offering to the town of Frankford, in remembrance of the happy days of his apprenticeship. It proved to be his last consecration of wealth to the glory of God.

In April, 1862, he purchased a lot on the corner of Main and Harrison Streets, about half a mile north of any evangelical church. Leaving about 100 feet square for the erection of a church when it should be needed, he commenced the chapel in 1865, and lived to see it nearly completed. It is one of the most beautiful models to be found in the suburbs of the city, built of the gray stone to be found in the immediate neighborhood. A few weeks previous to his death, feeling that he might not live to sign the title papers, he directed the grounds and chapel to be conveyed to the Trustees of the Presbyterian House, for the use of the congregation to be organized in this part of Frankford. Thus the last charity of his life was another characteristic anticipation of the future! Surely his works do follow him.

NOTHING now remains of our task but the grateful record of his declining years. They were overshadowed with continual suffering; but his hopes and purposes were ripening on every side. He was assured of success in business, beyond the reach of any calamities which could be foreseen. He was surrounded with the comforts and luxuries of his well-earned affluence. He had never suffered himself to withdraw capital from the business which was supporting so many families, and from the innumerable charities in which he was engaged, in order to increase his own comforts. But when these higher interests were secured, he felt justified in realizing his cherished dreams of a home in the country, where his rural and artistic tastes could be indulged. The site which he selected was most unpropitious; but it had an irresistible fascination for him. It was on the bank of the Delaware, a little above Frankford, where he had passed the years of his apprenticeship. Here he had taken his evening walks, when his labors were over, and looked out with wonder and hope upon his opening life. He had stood upon a little eminence overlooking marshy grounds and the broad river beyond, and dreamed of a life which should not be flooded with sins, nor suffered to lie waste like this desolation. And now, as a type of the success he had achieved, he resolved to redeem this waste land, and turn it into a beautiful garden. He excluded the river by a solid embankment; he drained the inclosure into two picturesque ponds, ornamented with miniature castles for the shelter of rare aquatic fowls. The flooding of these ponds by the tides was made to pump the water for the premises by an ingenious contrivance. The whole farm was laid out into a landscape of the most exquisite design: wild land was subdued; land was made where it was needed; luxuriant soil was supplied; the richest fruits and flowers were produced in profusion; an immense greenhouse kept the vegetation of the tropics in perennial bloom.

The mansion, which stands in the centre, was worthy of the place and the man. It is so symmetrical, and combines in itself such a variety

of designs, that its magnitude has no appearance
of ostentation: an air of simplicity and comfort
pervades the whole cluster of buildings within
the inclosure. And even the cottages of the
neighbors, which also belong to him, have been
built after a common design, so as to secure at
once variety and symmetry, so far as the eye can
reach.

In this beautiful home, within a few minutes'
ride of the city, he passed the summer months
of his declining years. But these were not
years of dignified repose. He was incessant in
his application to business. He was at his post
in the office, and unwearied in the inspection of
every part of his extensive works. And nearly
the whole of the work of church-building which
has been recorded in this narrative, was carried
on during these years of comparative rest.

A short time before the crisis of 1857, Mr.
Baldwin had some thoughts of retiring from
business. The crash came before he could
complete his arrangements. The same attempt
was renewed once afterwards, at a time of great
prosperity; but difficulties arose before it could
be carried out. He alluded to these facts afterwards, when asked why he continued his labors

when his age and infirm health would justify his retirement. "God has rebuked me," he said, "every time I have thought of repose. I believe he expects me to die in the harness." He did not struggle against the designs of Providence. He was a hard-working man to the last.

To his last days his most agreeable recreation from the excessive cares of business and charity was the exercise of ingenuity. He retained in the office the little vice and lathe, and all the tools employed in the jewelry business. He repaired the jewelry of his family with his own hands; and the machinery of a watch, taken apart and carefully assorted, was found in his drawer after death; showing how his last hours at the bench had been employed. He was always intent upon improving this indispensable article. He carried for many years a watch to which he had added a self-winding adjustment, and also a repeating apparatus of most ingenious construction. He was urged by those who were experienced in this trade, to secure a patent. But he exhibited his invention freely to the Swiss manufacturers, by whom it was greatly admired, and told them they were welcome to adopt any features of it which would be valuable. He had been well paid for his exertion in the recreation it had afforded him.

This favorite employment of spare hours arrested the attention of all who were ever admitted to his private office. "Whenever I called there," says Rev. E. E. Adams, D. D., "I found him in his little corner engaged in making some article of fancy or of utility—a spring, a wheel, a ring, repairing a knife, or a watch, or working out some delicate invention. On one occasion he was busily engaged in repairing, for a lady friend, a splendid inlaid table. Having a beautiful cane, the silver ring of which was worn out, I asked if he would like another job. He took the cane with a smile, and in a few minutes completed a new ring. This, to me, is a precious memento of his friendship and of his charming simplicity." The closing words of this communication from Dr. Adams have a touching interest from subsequent events; they show how early Mr. Baldwin began to fear that disease would silence that voice which had gathered by its own fascination the great congregation on Broad Street, and had influenced for good the whole community. " During the spring of 1866, he manifested great solicitude for my health, and insisted on taking me often to his own physician, in whose skill he had great confidence. It was a great grief to me that I did not earlier learn of his last illness, and have an interview with him once again before the silver cord was loosed and the golden bowl was broken. And now that he is no more among us, save by his hallowed influence, I miss, in common with others, the manly piety, the noble benevolence, and the burning patriotism which, as a halo of glory, crowned his life."

In the summer of 1860 he indulged himself in the only extensive tour of pleasure he ever enjoyed. He travelled over Great Britain and the continent of Europe. His interest was naturally excited by the improvements in machinery, and the application of science to the pursuits of industry. Still, he purposely forgot business as much as possible, and devoted most of his time and thoughts to the study of the rich treasures of art in the old country. His early tastes had now matured, and he added many gems to his extensive collection of rare paintings. But these fascinating pursuits were interrupted once by an alarming attack of the

19

disease from which he had been long suffering.
It was doubtful whether he would ever return.
But his own serenity was undisturbed. His only
anxiety was for those who would be mourners
in a strange land.

He returned home to find his country agitated
by the most intense political excitement which
he had witnessed during the whole of his eventful life. He was just commencing business for
himself when the Missouri Compromise introduced the question of American Slavery as the
controlling element of party organizations. He
finished his first locomotive when Disunion was
first threatened by the acts of nullification in
South Carolina. He was called from his busiest
labors upon the improved draft engines, to vote
upon the same question in the Constitutional
Convention of his State. During these forty
years, when so many of our best and wisest men
were groping after correct opinions, Mr. Baldwin had never had occasion to change his own.
It is no depreciation of those who have given
earnest heed to the solemn lessons of this dreadful conflict, to award higher praise to those who
were right from the beginning. The conservatives of 1837, the abolitionists of the last half

century, the radicals of to-day, have held their
ground unmoved by prejudice and denunciation;
they have been the moral instructors of this nation. God has vindicated their wisdom. Mr.
Baldwin was never a loud talker concerning
these or any other sentiments. We have seen
how he made them speak in his actions. No
considerations of popularity nor of his own interest could move him from the manly assertion
of his moral convictions. The fact is well
known that a rival company issued secret circulars, and sent them all over the South, at the
time when the prejudice against abolitionists
was at its height, denouncing him as one of the
most radical of them. Much of his business
was then at the South, where his machines were
always highly esteemed. His correspondents
wrote in the greatest alarm, to ask if the asser-
tions of this "black list" were true. His reply
was full of dignity and firmness. He denied
the right of any man to question him on political opinions in business transactions. "If I do
not fulfil my contracts, or if my work is not
satisfactory, your complaints are pertinent." But
rather than suffer his silence to be construed into
indifference to what he believed to be a moral

wrong, he gave them the most frank and courteous statement of his views.   His own interests
never exerted the slightest influence upon his
conscience.   Yet in this instance honesty proved
to be the best policy.   The falling off of his
southern orders began just in time to save him
from ruin by rebel repudiation.   His enemies
fell into the pit they digged for him.

But the Rebellion of 1861 afforded him the
opportunity for a still more emphatic expression
of his life-long convictions.   He received letters from a relative at the South, in violent denunciation of the principles which had just been
affirmed at the polls.   He replied at length, repeating the opinions he had always held, and in
the most spirited language, predicting their ulti-
mate triumph.   These letters, the only ones he
ever wrote in his life, of any public interest, are
probably destroyed.   They would be a treasure
indeed!   His zeal for the good cause, which
was now in peril, sometimes overcame his constitutional reluctance to appear in prominent
public positions.   He consented to preside at
patriotic meetings.   As chairman of the public
assembly which welcomed the brave colored
sailor, Robert Small, who carried the little

steamer *Planter* out of Charleston harbor during the war, he introduced him as "one worthy to be an admiral." It will be remembered that the city of Philadelphia, so justly praised for its patriotism and hospitality to the soldiers, suffered the ineffaceable shame of excluding this noble seaman from its public conveyances, on account of the color of his skin. Mr. Baldwin gladly accepted the invitation of his fellow-citizens to preside over another meeting called to protest against an outrage of this kind, and to assert the right of all men to the enjoyment of those public conveniences for which they are taxed. And he lived to see the principles he then defended, nobly enunciated by the President Judge of the Court of Common Pleas of Philadelphia.*

But this sense of justice, and unconscious superiority to the prejudices of his time, were not the fruits of any excitements growing out of the war. In this, as in everything else, he never followed, but always led public opinion. A fact in proof of this is well remembered by many of the older employees in the factory. Many

---

* A few months after his death the right to equal privileges in public conveyances was secured by an enactment of the Legislature of Pennsylvania.

years ago a colored man applied for work, and was employed at once in the boiler shop. The foreman in this department was one of the most valuable men in the whole works, and the position had always been a difficult one to fill. As soon as he saw the new recruit in his place he made a violent protest, and insisted upon his discharge.

"Certainly," was Mr. Baldwin's reply, "if he is not a good hand he shall be discharged on the spot."

The discontented man had too much justice to deny that he understood his business and worked faithfully.

"What, then, is your objection to him?"

"He is a *nigger*, and he must leave, or I will."

"Pack up, then, and be off with you."

There was no appeal from this decision. The foreman marched, and the negro kept his place till he died.

Mr. Baldwin loved the soldiers who were defending at once his country and his principles. He always had a friendly word for the brave men, and every effort for their comfort and spiritual good received his warmest sympathy and generous assistance. Besides the daily opportunities for private relief of suffering incident to the war, the books at the office show that immense sums were given away by the firm of M. W. Baldwin & Co. to the United States Sanitary and the Christian Commissions, and other organizations for the relief of the suffering soldiers of our grand armies and their families.

Mr. Baldwin took an early and especial part in the Sanitary Commission, an organization which accomplished more for the physical relief of the wounded soldiers in the late war than had ever before been accomplished in the history of warfare. He attended the first meeting of the Commission in Philadelphia on November 7th, 1861, and was an efficient member of the Executive Committee of the Philadelphia Associates from November 11th, 1861, the date of its formation, until his death, his attendance being regular, and his interest in the work of the Commission very marked.

In February, 1865, the Pastor of Calvary Church expressed, at a meeting of Session, the conviction that he ought to leave his work for a time, to preach to the soldiers, and labor with the Christian Commission for their comfort. Anticipating some reluctance on the part of the

Session to suffer their work to be interrupted, he was about to enlarge upon the needs of the army, and the revivals of religion in their encampments, when Mr. Baldwin broke in:—

"I move that the leave of absence be granted at once. Our pastors can do *us* more good in the field than at home."

He went; and came back, as thousands of other ministers came all over the land, to tell the wonderful story of God's blessing in the field, and to appeal for more money to help on the good work. As this meeting was in the evening, when Mr. Baldwin would be unable to be present, he took occasion to say to him in the afternoon:—

"I am going to beg for the Christian Commission this evening. You will not be there; but you know the story as well as I can tell it. I wish you would let me count in your contribution with the rest."

"I'm sorry to say this will be impossible," he replied; "for this is one of the objects to which my partner and I contribute from the Company funds, and he is absent. Tell Stuart to send round in a few days. However," he added, after a moment's reflection, "here is a trifle from my own pocket to put into the box to-night."

The trifle was One Thousand Dollars!

His love for the soldier made him very charitable in judging his faults. It is well known that he held for years the office of Inspector of the City Prison. The inspectors had the discretionary power of discharging persons under arrest for vagrancy, drunkenness, and petty offences. He was always inclined to the side of leniency, if justice were not to be sacrificed in the exercise of this power; but especially when he saw the bronzed face of a veteran in the motley throng, his sympathy was immediately excited.

"See that fine fellow! He's a soldier! There are some of the buttons on his coat yet. My dear boy," he would add, with a hand upon his shoulder, "you'll keep clear of the sharpies and the rum shops if we'll let you off this time, won't you?"

The simplicity of his tastes and generous impulses of his heart always restrained him from display in his domestic arrangements. After his business assumed the grand proportions of the Broad Street factory, he was often urged by

20

his friends to sell the Tenth Street house and
begin to live in the style of a man of fortune.
He resisted, and after the embarrassments of
1837, he met one of them with a smile of triumph, exclaiming: "How should I feel now,
selling my fine house, if I had taken your advice!" This caution in increasing personal ex-
penses should be considered by those who blamed
him for his indiscriminate charities. He regarded the slightest debt, incurred for his own gratification, as an' unwarrantable risk. But a note
of hand for thousands in the cause of beneficence
was only trusting God's promises. Nothing ever
distressed him so much as to be obliged to cur-
tail his charities. Even the comfortable house
on Spruce Street, which he purchased after his
fortune was made, had none of the ostentation
of affluence. And at last, in 1864, he made his
final move. He was then abundantly able to
build a marble monument to perpetuate his
name in one of the aristocratic precincts of the
city. But, to the surprise of every one, he purchased a substantial old-fashioned brick building
in the busiest part of Chestnut Street.

"Why should I banish myself from my fellow
creatures?" he said. "I have tried to live for

their good, and should I run away from them in my old age? I want to see the world, and have them see the things I enjoy, if it will afford them any pleasure or instruction."

This was the secret of his selection, as he confessed in private conversation afterwards.

"When I was a journeyman I used to enjoy looking at the prints and paintings exposed for sale. I think I acquired my first taste for art in this way. And sometimes, when I saw the top of a green-house over a high garden wall, I used to wonder why men wanted to hide the beautiful things which God made to be seen. I made up my mind then, that if I ever possessed any treasures of art or nature, I would give the journeymen a chance to enjoy them too!"

The time had come at last to realize his dream! He carried his rare paintings to the grand old house where all the world could find them easily. No one ever asked to "see the pictures" and was refused. He threw his magnificent parlors open every winter, to soirees of music, where the gems of the old masters were rendered.

"What a multitude of friends you are entertaining this evening!" a neighbor would say to him on such occasions.

"Yes; I never saw one in a dozen before, to my knowledge; but if they love to hear the symphonies of Beethoven played like that, they are all friends of mine."

But the crowning feature of the Chestnut Street house was a conservatory of rare flowers and tropical plants, which he fitted into the space between his house and the granite front of the Sunday School Union Depository. Here, on cold winter days, pine apples and oranges were ripening, and the richest flowers were in full bloom. The vapors were kept carefully wiped from the glass, and the plants were all arranged so as to be seen to the best advantage from the sidewalk. The first "opening" of this unique device caused a "sensation on Chestnut Street;" and scarcely a day passed without a crowd collected here from morning till night. The servants were annoyed a little by answering the bell for those who wanted to buy. But they were consoled when they saw how much happier their kind employer was, than any of the multitude on whom he conferred this pleasure. It was more blessed to give than to receive. The thankful looks from that endless procession, the letters of thanks which everybody wrote or desired to write, in return for this unique work

of beneficence, were among the sweetest joys of
his declining years.

But he was not satisfied with furnishing ra-
tional enjoyment to the masses. He longed to
have them all experience the blessings of the
Christian life. His religious zeal had never
been obtrusive, but always earnest and aggressive. And toward the close of life he became
more and more anxious to see souls coming to
the Saviour. He had never lost the revival spirit
of Dr. Skinner. The religious awakening of
1858 called forth his unwearied exertions and
unfaltering faith. Again in the spring of 1865
he rejoiced to see lost sinners finding refuge in
redeeming love. The sudden closing of the
Rebellion, and the bereavement of a whole people mourning for their father, seemed to hush
the nation with a stillness of religious awe and
expectation. Great revivals of religion followed
almost immediately in many parts of the country, and Philadelphia shared the blessing in some
measure. From the very first Mr. Baldwin was
outspoken in his approval of any measures which
the Spirit of God undoubtedly owned and blessed.
In this, as in everything else, he proved himself
superior to prejudice. It is well known that he

always approved of a more elaborate and artistic style of music than Christians generally find conducive to the devotional spirit. He did not believe in congregational singing in the Sabbath services. "I want the organ, and the most cultivated voices that can be obtained, to bear my soul to heaven, so that I cannot sing if I should desire." No one who enjoyed Mr. Baldwin's confidence could doubt that this style of music, which so often dissipates devotional feeling, was a means of grace to him. But the moment he saw that simpler melodies were winning souls to Christ, he forgot his own tastes, and joined with all his heart in singing "Come to Jesus." "There is neither poetry nor music in these songs," he used to say; "but what of that? the Holy Spirit is in them, and God has chosen the foolish things of this world to confound the wise." He never could bear to be asked whether he liked the manner of any zealous brother who was doing good. "Who am I to like or dislike? He is casting out devils in the name of Jesus. Woe is me if I forbid him because he follows not after me!"

He had long been prevented by his feeble health from attending the evening prayer meet-

ings of his church. But now a daily morning
prayer meeting was appointed, and for more
than two months he was always in his place,
urging the impenitent to seek salvation without delay. One of the most remarkable features of this work of grace was the eagerness of
inquirers to converse personally with Christians.
He often remained an hour after the meeting
to tell the story of the cross in simple and subdued tones, to burdened hearts. As Superintendent of the Sabbath School, his whole soul
was drawn out in prayer for the children. And
when a large number of them came to be received into the church, he welcomed them
heartily. He did not share the fears of many
good men, that young children would be incapable of comprehending and fulfilling the covenant of the church. "Jesus says, Suffer little
children to come unto me, for *theirs* is the kingdom of heaven. The church of Christ *belongs*
to the children." The feelings of his heart hit
upon the correct meaning of this text, which so
many learned men, like our translators, have
missed. And he always manifested the tenderest
interest, as an officer of the church, to cherish
and encourage the piety of these lambs of the
flock.

Thus his last days passed away in works of surpassing usefulness, in unexampled benevolence, and in unwearied labors in spiritual religion. He was a member of the Third Presbytery of Philadelphia in April, 1866, and repeated the testimony he had so often borne, in favor of a larger liberality, and a more spiritual mind, in the labors of the gospel. These were his last words to the Church of Christ: long may they be remembered!

His health was now rapidly failing. About this time the previous summer he had felt himself to be very near the grave. When he recovered, he expressed very freely, in conversation, the impressions he then experienced. He felt a natural shock at the near contemplation of death, but soon recovered the joys of full assurance. He had no desire to live. "The good works in which I am engaged must be carried on without my help very soon. The friends who love me cannot expect to retain me with them very long. Why should I desire to have my sufferings continued? If the will of God be so, it is better to depart and be with Christ." Yet he cheerfully accepted the duties of prolonged life. He went back to the "consecrated office" again. There he listened patiently to the many appeals for charities every day. He was always in his place on the Sabbath, in the Sabbath School and in the Session. He increased largely his contribution to every benevolent object. One of his last acts was to double his annual donation to the American Board of Commissioners for Foreign Missions.

But one day in June, 1866, he was observed to approach the office with a very feeble step. He tried to pursue his favorite employment, but he would drop the tools with a gesture of pain. The calls for donations seemed to be the only diversion which could make him forget his intense suffering. Early in the afternoon he left the scene of his labors and his success never to return. He went back to die in his home at Wissinoming.

21

THE summer passed in almost constant suffering of body, but in the peace of mind which passeth all understanding. On two occasions he enjoyed the pleasure of a visit from his lifelong friend, Rev. Mr. Barnes. In the grateful recollections of the past they almost forgot the approach of the king of terrors. It was only at the close of the final interview that Mr. Barnes lost his accustomed serenity, and threw his arms around his beloved friend, crying:

"O my brother, my brother, I cannot spare you yet!"

He came to console the afflicted; but he received consolation from the dying.

At six o'clock precisely, on the afternoon of Friday, September 7, 1866, just as the busy·hum of labor in his great manufactory ceased, he quietly sank to rest. There was a sublimity in the last scene which cannot be described. Surrounded with a profusion of everything which made life desirable, he was surrendering life without regret. The breath of summer came into his beautiful mansion, freighted with the perfume of the rare flowers his hand had planted, and the songs of the birds his forest of beauty had invited. From the window he could look over the broad acres which had been redeemed from desolation, so suggestive of the multitudes who had been raised from misery by his beneficence.

But when these recollections of a well-spent life were suggested as a ground of consolation in the present trial, his face would brighten with a far more precious recollection. "All of grace! all of grace! God has given me great opportunities for doing good. But the disposition to do good was something still better. This I owe to the grace of God, in Jesus Christ my Saviour."

There was no transport in the last hour. He had never been subject to the vicissitudes of excited feeling. Habitual calmness and repose reigned supreme in his spirit throughout his eventful life. His last struggle was equally free from the extremes of pain and of rapture. In perfect peace, and undisturbed confidence in the mercy of God, he fell asleep in Jesus.

No words can express the grief and conster-

nation which the announcement of this event
caused throughout the community. That he
was a great sufferer was well known. But he
had engaged in such extensive works of beneficence since his infirmities had confined him to
the house for the greater part of every summer,
that more enlarged plans of usefulness than ever
before, had been undertaken in confident reli-
ance upon his support. And now in a moment
this "pillar in the Temple of God" had fallen!
In the first tumult of distress for our own irreparable loss, we may be forgiven for not reflect-
ing that the pillar was not fallen, only transferred
to a fairer temple on high, whence he should
go no more out; on him was now written the
name of God, and the name of the city of God,
of the New Jerusalem which cometh down from
heaven, even Jesus' own new name. For, alas!
we had no ear then to hear what the Spirit said
to the churches!

Farewell, brave, beautiful life! It was like a
clear and bounteous river, which, encountering
obstacles in its course, finds new and enlarged
channels, and supplies nourishment to broad
wastes of land, while it loses nothing of the
purity and the abundance of its own waters.

But, alas! it has disappeared out of our sight,
like the streams of the East which suddenly
sink into the sands of the desert. A desert, indeed, will this life appear to multitudes without
the bounties of his hand and the priceless sympathy of his loving heart.

Can we suffer so much good to perish out of
this world utterly? Shall all the virtues of the
Christian life form the subject of his epitaph
and the magnificence of his tomb? Shall the
affection which followed him all his life strive
in vain bewilderment to be his companion in
death? Shall our grateful hearts be his mauso-
leums?

Oh, not in dead hearts must such a name be
cherished! Let life, and courage, and hope, and
faith be the offerings we bring to his memory.
Let us turn from the oppressive contemplation
of the dead to adoring trust in Him who was
dead and is alive, and behold He liveth for ever-
more, that from the fountain of His everlasting
grace we may receive those virtues which we
have now admired, and enter into that inheritance which made the day of our mourning the
day of his glory and triumph!

THE DEATH OF GOD'S PEOPLE

NO LOSS

TO GOD'S CHURCH.

A SERMON,

OCCASIONED BY THE

DEATH OF MATTHIAS W. BALDWIN,

AT HIS RESIDENCE NEAR FRANKFORD,

SEPTEMBER 7, 1866.

PREACHED IN ST. MARK'S CHURCH, FRANKFORD, SEPTEMBER 9, 1866,
BY THE RECTOR, REV. D. S. MILLER, D. D.

"Help, Lord, for the godly man ceaseth, for the faithful fail from among the children of men."—PSALM XII. 1.

THESE words of the Psalmist have found an echo in the hearts of God's people, in all their generations to this day, whenever it has pleased Him to take his eminent servants to Himself. The Church in the midst of the evil world, is forced against the higher spiritual judgment of the believer to depend more upon human instrumentalities than becomes the calling unto God through Jesus Christ, and lives too much by sight and not by faith. But God has done all his great work for his people and his service by the *men* he has sent upon his Missions; and when He invests them with his favor and blesses

22

them in all they do, and by their labors increases, upholds, and defends his Fold, they that are the sheep of his pasture are easily led to fear when these sources of their comforts are withdrawn, when the means of their defence are withheld, and they are left alone without accustomed Guards and Guides.

These remarks are suggested by the event which has occurred within a few hours, in our own vicinity, in the death of Mr. Baldwin. He had achieved by his talent, his successful skill, and his still increasing fortune, a power and a place among us in this city, which all will acknowledge; and he used these advantages, not in the way of sin and of mere selfish pleasure, but for the good of others, in great part, and for the glory of God. He honestly and fairly paid the tribute of his wealth and name to his Maker; and he was known not more widely as a successful manufacturer and a wealthy citizen than as a Christian, a member of Christ's Church, and as one who professed to go in the way of good rather than evil. Now, as place and power are of immense influence over men, and used for sinful ends, make fearful mischief among us, hindering the good and hardening the wrong, it is a singular blessing when they fall into the hands of the godly; and it is not strange that Christians should mourn when such as these die and are no longer able to wield their influence for God. The command of men which belongs to extensive manufacturing operations, such as Mr. Baldwin was engaged in, is a fearful talent when used to encourage sin: how can we feel anything but regret when he who made it a blessing ceases to rule. The name which such as he wins among his neighbors and fellow-citizens, a name coupled with the possession of costly residences, expensive luxuries, skill in a notable profession, and large wealth, such a name if held as a synonym for vice or dishonor, is a potent agent for Satan; but when, as in the case of Matthias W. Baldwin, it stood for Religion, for Benevolence, for God's Honor, for Sunday-School teaching, for the care of the poor, the sick, and the ignorant, for building of Houses of God, then it is something for Christians to be thankful for while they have it, and to mourn over when God takes it away.

The common life of every man makes up a gospel of sin or salvation which reads like a New Testament commentary in a Christian age.

But more particularly is it so when the history is that of a progress from small to great means; a growth in talent, repute, skill, wealth, and usefulness, and when finally it is all consecrate to God, like the Cross topping the pile and devoting it to holy ends. Mr. Baldwin was at one time a resident in this vicinity, practising his first art on this very street, a young man without other means than a true head, heart, and hands. Here he married and began the world. But he is known to us now by a great and tasteful mansion, and by all the appliances of position and large fortune. He has won his way from the one to the other by God's blessing, by God's aid. This has been a divine purpose. We know it must be so, for this was a godly life, and God watches the good man's way; and because of the use which was made of these distinctions, for only the Holy Spirit is the author of our good deeds. It was therefore a divine purpose, this life for a divine end; it was a city set upon a hill, that by its shining for Him, men might see the good light and glorify the Father in heaven.

Thus in the very enumeration of our losses by the death of God's special servants, we see how He answers our prayer and helps us. Help, Lord, for the godly man ceaseth. We are taught that *God was in all their lives,* and in all that they were permitted to do. Thus we have a strong additional proof that He is in His church, and doing his work. One of the wheels in the divine machine has been removed; but ever since it began to revolve we see that it has been governed by the great Master's hand; and that is just as present now in this last motion by which the instrument has been taken out of our sight, as in all before. The Ruler is revealed by the absence of His servant. We may be in doubt what shall next happen. Whether the good work which the lost servant has done shall be continued, whether another shall take his place; but we have no doubt that *God is here,* and therein we rest content.

But God has a thousand times proven to us that His work suffers no loss by the death of His eminent servants. Moses goes and He sends Joshua. Or, far better, no Joshua comes, but out of the tribes who, as they feared, had lost their all when Moses was withdrawn, rise up little ones, who do the very work which has been abandoned; and for one great servant taken away, the Lord has scores, like the monster of fable, with heads still growing as they are cut away. Ofttimes in the life and labors of one earnest and useful man, others grow sluggish, and look only to him. The Master takes away their support and they are either scourged out of the vineyard, because manifestly incapable; or they awake to strength and vigor they never knew before, and watch and struggle, and exceed the hand they mourned for.

But there are some blessed thoughts connected with the death of God's important servants, which make their dying more fragrant for us than their lives. There might be some doubt as to the functions in the future of ordinary believing men who die, but those who have always *labored* here must labor there. God has never ceased to make use of them in this world. He will not drop a tool of his own choosing in the world beyond. Hence we know the blessed truth, that God has fields of service beyond the present. There, with minds unlimited, with fathomless hearts, with years that do not cease, the blessed saints of God shall work for him forever. Far, far down the countless ages stretches the holy harvest, and those who love the Saviour shall gather it for Him. Oh! it is a priceless promise for the limbs beginning to ache, and the life growing weary, of the poor toilers in God's acre here. There the work is to begin anew and never to end; to begin and never to fail; to go on and never to weary; and Jesus always by to smile, and encourage, and reward.

But we learn beside, that He will not suffer his holy saints to be overburthened and broken down utterly. No! he takes them *home* when they are weary, no matter what may be the cost. O how long our foolish, faithless hearts would hold fast to those we need, had we the dispensation of their fate. Would our hearts ever let them go whom we love? Could we ever spare those who fight, and work, and give for us, and never hold back their hands or lives in our need? Ah! but their God is tenderer and breaks them from our clinging. He says "Come," to the burdened man, and smooths the pillow of eternal rest and bids him lay there. He says "Come," to the exhausted watcher, and opens to him the heavenly heights of vigor and growth, where labor has no fatigue and work is delight. All men long for the hour of repose, here or hereafter. Sick of the world, of miserable false men, of disappointments and losses, we yearn for rest. Is there any sweeter lesson in the death of God's people than that it is to give them this? No matter who loses, no matter how mourned over or needed, the Master cares for his own. He has spoken it. They shall have their REST!

And thus we get a sweet ideal of Heaven. One by one, He has taken them thither whom we knew. Their goodness, their zeal, their love, their labor, their Christly life—what bright particular stars they were here, as we saw them each by each! But there! gathered into one—one perfect glorious constellation—of its beauty, and its glory, and its eternal brightness we could frame no fancy had not our saintly ones died—died as we knew them. But *he* is in it, and *he*, and *she*; Mary and Martha, John and Peter! Lord, it *must* be a goodly land, on which those who were so holy and precious here, forever shine. How near it seems, filled with those so familiar and so worthy in our eyes here. The veil is lifted up and the door opened when we remember all we loved and wondered at in the lives of God's people while they were with us, and when we see that they are still at work for the same Lord on high. Heaven and earth are one. The Church above and the Church below have

the same company and the same employments.
But we have not *done with them*, God's greater servants, when they have passed from us; nor have
they ceased to bless us, for though they be dead,
they have left to us their memory and their work.
This last lies all about us wherever we have seen
them labor, or know they would have labored.
And there is this truth especially for us, in reference to their work, that now WE can do more
at it than the greatest of them who are gone.
Therefore we, in all our humbleness and imper-
fection, are more necessary to God for this than
they. He has dispensed with their labor. He
has no need for it. It is of no use to him. But
us he does need. He cannot and will not do
without us, for he has taken them away, and left
us standing before the unfinished labor. Take
heart, then, O feeble son, and seize the father's
plough! Take courage, O daughter, and carry
on his ministering. Labor, brother, it is the
Lord's call, and where He calls he gives strength
also.

And to encourage us to do what they have
left undone, we have their memory. It is their
best legacy. Fortunes take wings and go; good
works die like all mortal things; houses decay

23

and tumble into dust; but the recollections of a life of industry, earnestness, brave struggle, untiring assiduity, and perfect integrity, *do not die*, they become part of our common lives. Above all do a conscientious, loving, faithful Christian walk and conversation, a life hid with Christ in God, dwell with us, shape our consciences, cheer and encourage us, and by the noble striving, and the nobler heavenly end, teach us to live also, and to labor also, looking to Jesus and making our most precious monument in the hearts sanctified and souls saved of those who, like this their copy, followed on to know the Lord.

OBITUARY NOTICE

OF

MATTHIAS W. BALDWIN.

BY THE

HON. JOSEPH R. CHANDLER.

MATTHIAS W. BALDWIN.

From the North American and United States Gazette, September 14, 1866.

IF it was a good and a wholesome thought in
"Old Mortality" to deepen and keep legible
the inscriptions upon the tombstones of those
who had honored their country or their religion,
and thus to keep alive their memories, they are
little less entitled to good consideration who
first chiselled those names, and· placed on stone
a record of the virtues that reflected credit on
their possessor, and produced a desire to imitate
the admitted excellence.   Hence benefits are
conferred upon society when mention is made
of the excellence of those whose lives have illustrated the virtues that belong to their condition, and whose deaths have done honor to their
profession.

The death of our late townsman, Matthias
W. Baldwin, has been mentioned in all the daily
papers of our city, and reference has been made

to the means by which he acquired his position in business, and became the master of princely wealth. The lesson of Mr. Baldwin's life, even in that regard, must be profitable to the young, who are considering how they may ascend; and a minute notice of the particular steps which lead on to fortune would be instructive to all who are seeking encouragement in their efforts to achieve a place. Not less, nay even more so, would be a fair statement of the difficulties encountered in the selection of means and the judgment evinced in the abandonment of those that did not, on trial, equal expectation, and the still greater judgment that comprehended in advance the movements of the times and provided a supply of that which was only about to be needed.

The foresight of Mr. Baldwin, his promptness to seize upon the suggestion of a sound judgment, and his patient abiding of the harvest of a liberal sowing and careful culture, his buoyant hopes amid difficulties and his admirable use of success are instructive, and should be made familiar to the young. They are a part of the jewels of our city, as they are illustrations of the character of our people.

But the writer of this is unskilled in those ennobling acts by which Mr. Baldwin achieved his great distinction as a manufacturer. He leaves, therefore, to others, who comprehend the difficulties of the trade, and the high genius by which those difficulties were surmounted, to give the instructive lesson which they ought to convey, and make Matthias W. Baldwin the subject of a volume that shall be to the young mechanic and merchant their "Best Companion."

Fifty years' acquaintance with Mr. Baldwin, and frequent association with him in the discharge of public duties, enable the writer to speak of him as a *conscientious man;* and in that ennobling quality lay the secret of his great success. What he undertook, he believed to be right. What he said, he knew or believed to be true. What he completed bore upon it no less the mark of a master mind and master hand than an impress of strong moral integrity, and a well-regulated conscience. If Mr. Baldwin was seen in his earlier days connecting new business with that which he had first undertaken; or if he started the boiler manufactory by passing from one pursuit to another, time served to show that he was reaching out to that means of

distinction for which his genius and skill had
fitted him, and making himself ready, by taking
a first step, to take those which his progress
should suggest. His new views were attained
by ascending, and his foothold was made secure
on each attainment by the correctness of his
judgment.

He who leads public enterprise must sometimes wait the progress of the many, or be left
alone. He who provides in advance for others
may often find his provision neglected and his
hopes disappointed. Mr. Baldwin understood
that from experience; but when he became a
public benefactor by anticipating the large demand for locomotive engines, his enterprise and
judgment were rewarded by that success which
is the artisan's great object, and finally by that
wealth which is the almost certain result of
foresight and enterprise, directed by sound judgment and a pure conscience.

A suggestive theme for a public address or an
essay might be found in the business abilities,
character, and success of Mr. Baldwin; and
some one who would make the lesson attractive
will probably present it to the young, as an encouragement to undertake with prudence great

matters, and pursue with earnestness whatever their hands find to do, and not to be deterred by small obstacles, and especially not to cease from enterprise because a single path to success has been closed. There is a power in genius that moulds events to its own purposes, or accommodates itself to new circumstances. It is certainly good for any man who has to achieve his own pecuniary independence, that his taste and education should be moulded to the requirements of a pursuit upon which he is to enter. But it is better that his powers of mind should be so directed that he may seize upon new suggestions, and profit by a change which chance or progress may make. The discoveries of science, the inventions of genius, and the advancement of the arts, are constantly presenting new objects for enterprise, upon which men of character in their pursuits may seize, and make them subservient to immense success. Mr. Baldwin comprehended that, and he profited by the changes which railroads produce, and rose to distinction upon a business that had no existence when he commenced business life.

Mr. Baldwin then was prominent in his occupation. He understood the art which he prac-

24

tised, and he knew how to make science subservient to that art, and so he became great as a business man. But the distinction and wealth which Mr. Baldwin acquired were less to him than that serenity of temper by which the hours of business or of social enjoyment were illuminated; and the wealth which he acquired seemed chiefly valuable to him as a means of gratifying a refined taste, and promoting objects worthy the consideration of an immortal mind. The writer of this article had the pleasure of observing the progress of Mr. Baldwin for fifty years, of sharing with him public responsibilities; and no act, even in his most straitened day, is recalled on which Mr. Baldwin was less a true and upright man than he was when no temptations but wealth invited him to swerve. He was in principle an honest man. There was no necessity for thought, for calculation, to make him do right—right with him was almost an instinct, so deeply seated and so constantly active was such a principle. He was a good man.

To the young, Mr. Baldwin seemed to die in a good old age; to his contemporaries and his seniors, he seemed to have been called away in the midst of that soundness of judgment which

great experience matures, and in the fulness of
that intellect which was so useful to others.

Mr. Baldwin's strong sense of right made him
tenacious of the principles which he had adopted, and upon which his public and private life
was moulded. He was firm in his adherence to
them, and, at proper seasons, he was earnest in
their defence, though rather conspicuous in their
illustration. But he never wounded the sensi-
bilities of others by an untimely presentation of
his own views, nor outraged the proprieties of
social life by indelicate attacks upon the opposing
opinions of associates. Stern in the practice of
those virtues which belong to the religion which
he professed, he was yet most lenient to the errors which marred the character of others. He
cautioned the erring with delicacy, and he rebuked the offender with gentleness. For lesser
faults he had the forbearance of one who understood the weakness of human nature, and for
graver offences he had the censure that startles
but mends. To the young man who had departed slightly from the way, he extended a
hand that led to the right; for the older he had
a pardon and a blessing that bade him go and
sin no more.

No one can tell into how many channels the good influences of Mr. Baldwin extended. His liberal hand was open to assist the unfortunate, and to direct, by example, the character of others. His own life and its results were to the younger an encouragement to virtuous enterprise, while his own vast undertakings gave active and profitable employment to hundreds who lived in the influence of his good example, and grew better in an atmosphere of the purest morals that Christianity has softened and sanctified.

The ruling motive of Mr. Baldwin's action was *right*, not merely the abstract sense of right that permits no direct wrong to others, but that higher, purer sense, that made him solicitous that all the enjoyment which he had of his own right should be multiplied by and ministered to the good of others. Hence, it was a rule of life with him to multiply the rights of others, that he might increase their usefulness and their enjoyment.

All who knew Mr. Baldwin knew him to be a zealous Christian. The best qualities of religion were illustrated by his unostentatious charities, his large philanthropy, his love for man. All who knew Mr. Baldwin could not designate the denomination of Christians with which he had direct and intimate fellowship; but a man of such fixed principles would scarcely be without an explicit creed, and with an attachment so strong and so particular as to make him seek to extend the benefits of his general views by means of the channels which he held to be most appropriate. No man that approached Mr. Baldwin with requests for means to promote any good object ever went away empty; but who can tell how full-handed returned those who intimated to him the necessities of some religious enterprise that was directly on the way which he specially approved. The largest of these offerings are known. The liberal man shuts his eyes to the evidence of his liberality, but the beneficiary suffers an open mouth to speak out of the abundance of a grateful heart.

The Master and Teacher of all benevolence did not rebuke the presentation of a motive for prayer for the restoration of a sick man, "That he hath builded us a synagogue." He might have heard the reason urged with double force in behalf of one whose death is now mourned, and whose life may have been protracted by the exercise of those graces which strengthen where they influence and bless the objects upon which they are employed.

No man in this city, perhaps, has ever done more for the religious denomination of which he was a member than was necessarily known to be done by Mr. Baldwin. The thousand percolating drops of incidental aid, the numerous rills of charity that flowed from his ample means are to be judged of only by the blessings which they produced, the benefit of the individual or the association alone "betraying the secret of their silent course." But there are others, where princely munificence, moved by a religious discrimination, meet the eye and command the respect of those who know how doubly beneficial is that aid which comes at a moment of need. The record of such liberality is made where it will be ineffaceable. The character and deeds of the man capable of such acts will be held in "sweet remembrance."

Mr. Baldwin, though always alive to the interests of the country, found little time for what is called public positions. He was a member of the Convention that formed the present Constitution of the State of Pennsylvania; and his influence was given to the conservative side of measures discussed. He was at the time of his death, and had been for many years past, a member of the Board of Inspectors of the Philadelphia County Prison, in which situation his business habits, and his sense of justice, and his love of mercy, made him eminently useful, while the urbanity of his manners secured for him the affectionate esteem of his colleagues.

No one could attempt an analysis of the character of Mr. Baldwin without being struck with its wonderful, its beautiful simplicity, and the adaptation of his manner to all with whom he came into relation. The humblest artisan found in him a sympathizing friend, and the noblest and boldest projector felt instructed by his observation. The aged gathered encouragement by his presentation of the benefits of his experience, and children grew happy in his benignant smiles. He seemed to have a force of character that took him through all enterprises, and a gentleness of disposition that gave sunshine to all results. The extended factory and the ponderous machinery seemed to be trifling instruments in his hands to effect great objects; while home, the fireside, with its splendid collection of the fine arts, and the endearing smile of affection that no art could make or imitate, was the sanctuary of the domestic affections.

It is for others to do more ample justice to the character of Mr. Baldwin, and tempt the young aspirant for distinction, by showing how truth, conscientiousness, and persevering industry secure success, and how the best instincts of the human heart and the purest principles of religion are compatible with the most devoted attention to the business of life; how, indeed, they influence the plans and direct the execution of the schemes of the man of enlarged enterprise, and finally, how they gain predominance and become the leading motive where they had only been the influencing power.

Some one else will find time to show how much honor the creative and completing faculties of such a man as Mr. Baldwin reflect on his whole country; how the fulfilment of his great undertakings is made a blessing to others, who in a hundred ways are called on to perform part of the immense labor for which his inventive power created a demand; and how the city in which he dwelt feels that the fame, the character, and the success of Matthias W. Baldwin are inseparable and valuable portions of her civic honors. Let it be the object of this article to show that in Philadelphia such a man as Matthias W. Baldwin could not live without the distinction which talent, enterprise, success, and purity of life ought to secure, and such a man could not die without the regret that so much worth should pass away, nor without gratitude to God that the highest honors which our city has to bestow are reserved for the man who is faithful to his vocation, and in all his relations an example of noble, generous enterprises and of gentle, Christian manners.

25

MEMORIAL

OF

MATTHIAS W. BALDWIN.

BY

FRANKLIN PEALE.

MEMORIAL.

Read before the American Philosophical Society of Philadelphia, at a meeting held on the Seventh day of December, A. D. 1866.

THE life of a man, like that of the subject of this notice, furnishes a vast amount of matter, and exemplifies the results of character, habits, and principles that are most useful in their influences on all classes of society, and in all the relations of life; but the usages of this Society do not authorize details, however desirable upon other accounts, or however interesting to the immediate relatives of the departed; a just record of the life and character of the deceased is all that is aimed at in this Memorial.

On the tenth day of December, 1795, in Elizabethtown, New Jersey, Matthias William Baldwin was born. Much the largest proportion of his life was passed in the city of Philadelphia, in the vicinity of which, at his country seat, Wissinoming, he died, on the evening of

September 7th, 1866, in the seventy-first year of his age.

He was the son of William Baldwin, and an exemplary mother, whose influence on his future life was all that could be desired, in moral and religious example and precept.

He had the misfortune to lose the first in early childhood, but the judicious training and industrious energy of the last so far supplied the loss that no serious privation followed in the rearing of a family of five children, two of whom survive at this time.

His father was in life successful in a mechanical profession, and realized property, which was subsequently lost, thus calling forth the energy of his mother, as previously noticed; it is therefore obvious how the mechanical tendencies of the subject of this notice had their origin; and accordingly the occupations and amusements of the boyhood of Matthias were mechanical, in which he indulged as far as time and limited means permitted.

His education under such circumstances was necessarily confined to the ordinary acquirements of elementary instruction, which after-studies and associations much improved and enlarged.

The profession chosen for him, to which he was apprenticed, was that of jeweller, in the obligations of which he was faithfully occupied during the five years of his minority, in Frankford, Pennsylvania.

After this he was employed in the establishment of Fletcher and Gardener, in this city, extensive manufacturers and dealers in jewelry and plate. The first named being subsequently one of the officers of the Franklin Institute, in which Institution Mr. Baldwin exercised an active and influential part, as will be noticed hereafter.

Mr. Baldwin commenced business on his own account in 1819, in the manufacture of jewelry, and appears to have been successful for a limited time only, as he subsequently changed his business to the manufacture of bookbinders' tools, calico-printers' rolls, &c., in which he became associated with Mr. David Mason. In this business the enlarged views of Mr. Baldwin and his careful manipulation were eminently important, and the results such as usually accompany skilled, practical ability. Thus associated, a manufactory was established, beginning in the year 1825, that rendered the country independent of foreign supply. It was situated in a small street, run-

ning north from Walnut Street, above Fourth
Street, in this city. It was in this place that the
author of this memoir made the acquaintance of
Mr. Baldwin, which afterwards ripened into an
intimacy that continued in uninterrupted har-
mony to the end of his life.

The success of the firm in the departments
just noticed, and the increase of business arising
from it, induced a change of locality to a larger
space, and increased power; it was effected by
removal to Minor Street near Sixth, in the latter
part of 1827, or beginning of 1828, and it was
here that the dawn of his prosperity had its rise,
to shine forth a bright and glorious noon of
utility and success.

It was in this workshop that Mr. Baldwin
made the designs for, and built his first steam-
engine, intended to supply the motive power
demanded by his enlarged business. It was of
novel construction, in several respects, and was
finished to an extent entirely unexampled in that
day. Its vertical cylinder, so placed for economy
of space; its forked cross-head and pitman,
guides at the sides of the cylinder, were novel-
ties, in the disposition and form of parts, and its
bevel wheels, which gave motion to the gover-

nor, were without teeth, doing their duty by friction alone, being noiseless, like the beautiful engine whose motion that governor controlled.

This little engine of five-horse power was the object of much attention among machinists, and excited general admiration by its quiet, though efficient motion, and the fine finish of all its parts. It is at this hour an efficient motive power in the great establishment of M. W. Baldwin & Co., with very slight changes in its parts, a durable evidence of the sound mechanical judgment of him who designed and executed it.

It was about this time that the attention of the world was concentrated on the importance of railroads for transportation, and the means of moving upon them. The history of the locomotive is well known, and need not be recapitulated; but the experience in this country was very limited, although the public mind and curiosity were ardently drawn towards all that had been done, or was doing in relation thereto. It was in consequence of the feeling on this important matter that Mr. Baldwin was requested by the author of this memoir to make for the Philadelphia Museum—of which he was manager—a

26

model locomotive. After the examination of all the resources then available in description, and sketches of the engines which had competed for the premium on the Liverpool and Manchester Railroad, a plan was adopted, and the model engine commenced in 1830, and after a few experiments and modifications, finished in 1831, and on the 25th of April of that year was put in operation on a track laid in the rooms of the Museum, in the Arcade, making the circuit of the whole suite, and drawing two miniature cars, containing seats for four passengers (which were sometimes loaded double), in a manner highly gratifying to the public, who attended in crowds to witness—for the first time in this city and State—the effect of steam in railroad transportation.

It may be proper to observe that the efficiency of this miniature engine, and its satisfactory performance, were mainly due to the discharge of the exhaust, or waste steam, into the stack, or chimney—a principle of vital importance in all engines, rendering a blowing apparatus unnecessary, and supplying the fuel with air requisite for combustion, without the sacrifice of power for that object, a principle then new, or little known in this connection. To whom the invention (if it can be so called) is due, who at this time can tell? The fuel used in the small fire space of the boiler of this model was pine-knot coal, although anthracite was partially successful in its application, the difficulty in the use of any fuel being the diminutive space above alluded to.

It may be permitted also, in this connection, to observe that the first published observations upon the foaming of water in boilers, were made in the use of this model. They may be found in one of the newspapers of the day.

The attention of machinists was drawn to the subject of locomotion with considerable energy about this time. It was one of the great movements of the epoch; it demanded and received the attention the necessities of commerce and general intercourse required. Mr. Baldwin, as it may be naturally inferred, shared in the general excitement, and was therefore prepared to undertake the task, when an order came in 1832 from the Philadelphia and Germantown Railroad Company for the construction of a locomotive for that Company's road.

The only examples or information previous to this time of the construction of the now per-

fected locomotive engine, were the crude efforts
of the previous years, and the various published
and imperfect accounts and illustrations in the
journals of the day.

Mr. Baldwin and the writer inspected the de-
tached parts of a locomotive imported by the
Camden and Amboy Railroad Company, in a
shed on their road near Bordentown (at least
such is the recollection of the place), and under
some difficulty succeeded in making such observations and a few measurements as were thought
would be of service.   It was with these slender
means of observation, and the limited experience
of the preceding model, that the task was undertaken, and the execution of the order commenced.   It is but justice to add that it was
accompanied by restrictions as to weight that
are now at variance with all the principles that
are desired, in fact, govern, the use of motive
power on railroads.

The building of this engine was carried on
under the difficulties of few and insufficient
tools and space, and completed in about six
months. Begun in Minor Street, it was finished,
in 1832, in the new and larger space in Lodge
Alley, to which the shop had been removed,

and was placed upon the road on the 23d of November in that year.

The experiments which were immediately made with the "Ironsides," as this engine was called, in speed and management were eminently successful. The writer and other friends, scientific and mechanic, made short excursions on the road, realizing the sensations that only occur once in a generation, under the novel circumstances afforded by, as in this case, the flight through the air at the rate of fifty or sixty miles an hour.

Difficulties arose in the settlement of his account with the officers of the Company, who appear to have expected that this engine would do what their own restrictions had rendered impossible; and there were other difficulties that had their origin in the grading and construction of the road itself.

These facts are amusingly illustrated by one of the advertisements of the Company, which was in the following words :—

"NOTICE.—The engine (built by Mr. Baldwin) with a train of cars, will run daily (commencing this day), when the weather is fair, as follows," &c. . . . "*When the weather is not fair,* the horses will draw the cars the four trips."

No one need be told now that when the rails are wet there is less adhesion than at other times, and as the grades were steep, it is not surprising that one of the lightest engines ever built, was unable to draw all the cars, and all the crowd that panted for a trip by steam. The parties who indulged such unreasonable desires could not have exercised common reason in expecting from the motive power more than was witnessed by the writer, the slipping of the wheels under a full head of steam.

The sand-box, now an indispensable adjunct of every locomotive, was then unknown; had it been, it would most likely have supplied the means of adhesion, something better than the horses' feet, advertised to guarantee the trip.

This little engine was an undoubted success, and subsequently, when fairly and skilfully run on the road, properly adjusted and secured, gave entire satisfaction to the public, and all parties concerned.

The removal to enlarged premises in Lodge Alley, gave facilities that soon told upon his reputation, and augmented his business; in this place his second engine was made, and successive numbers undertaken. Further increase of busi-

ness rendered another removal necessary; in
1835, the property at the corner of Broad and
Hamilton Streets was purchased, and here the
regular manufacture of Locomotives, on an enlarged scale, was established, and became the
principal occupation, although it did not exclude
other business, as evidenced by the construction
of the engine for the City Ice Boat, whose
efficient services in clearing the channel of the
Delaware, as well as her employment by Government during the late rebellion, are well
known to the whole community.

It is not necessary to enumerate the various
improvements made by Mr. Baldwin, in the
parts, construction, and manufacture of Locomotives; it would be a lengthy enumeration.
It is sufficient to say, that the results are seen on
all the railroads of the country, in the presence
of engines adapted to all the purposes of draught
and speed.   But a passing remark, reverting to
past history, upon the fact of ascending the
inclined plane at Belmont, and manœuvring
upon it, was one of the feats of that early date,
exciting surprise in the minds of all, whether
natural philosopher, mechanician, or ordinary
observer.   Since that day, the mountain heights

of our coal fields, even the Alleghany ridge itself, seem to offer scarcely any impediment, either to the ponderous engine, or its cumbrous train of freight. Much of this success in transportation is due to the form and adaptation of the best freight engines, which have had their origin in the magnificent establishment of M. W. Baldwin & Co., in this city.

It must not be supposed that the career thus imperfectly sketched, was an uninterrupted course of prosperity; on the contrary, it was attended by financial and other embarrassments, that at times were nearly fatal in their effects; but it is equally true that Mr. Baldwin's confidence in his own ability, and the line that he was pursuing, never failed, and it is well known that his integrity, appreciated and regarded as it was, kept and sustained him through all the convulsions of those days, and ultimately crowned his success with the halo of honor, under which he met and extinguished every debt, both principal and interest.

It might reasonably be supposed, that with such a weight of responsibilities, Mr. Baldwin was fully occupied with the conduct of his Factory; he found time, nevertheless, to take a full share of the duties of a member and officer of the Franklin Institute of this State. He was one of the original members, participating in the proceedings of March the 20th, 1824; was placed on the Committee of Science and Arts in 1834; elected Vice-President in 1855, and so remaining until 1863.

In the examination of machines and inventions presented to the judgment of the Institute, he was always distinguished for the sound views he took of principles, and keen insight of the merit of the article presented, and candid and independent in his opinions and statements in relation thereto.

He had the honor of election to the American Philosophical Society, on the 18th of January, 1833, and was often present at its meetings, though rarely taking an active part in its proceedings.

The Horticultural Society of this city was a favorite institution; he contributed largely to the attractiveness of the meetings, by a liberal display of the beauties of his conservatory, and presided over its affairs for a number of years. He was elected a member March 18th, 1851, and was elevated to the Presidency, January

27

19th, 1858, in which office he continued until 1863.

The resolutions which were adopted by the members, on the announcement of his decease, were of the most grateful, appreciative, and regretful character.

A peculiar fondness for foliage in color and form was one of his characteristic traits, at least such a deduction may justly be drawn, from the number and variety of the strange though beautiful leaves of plants which his conservatories contained.

Mr. Baldwin was also a member of the Board of Directors of the Pennsylvania Academy of the Fine Arts. Elected to that body in the year 1852. The appreciation of his associates in the Direction of that Institution is demonstrated by the resolutions adopted by them on the announcement of his separation from their association.

Mr. Baldwin became a member of the Musical Fund Society, founded for the support of decayed musicians and the promotion of the art, although the increase of population, and the consequent resources of the musical portion of the community have long since rendered the second object of the corporation (in which it had been eminently successful) no longer a necessity; yet Mr. Baldwin, while health permitted, never failed to give his presence and countenance to the duties of the first object, and the obligations of the committees on which he was placed. He became an amateur member April 27th, 1847, and a life member October 6th, 1852, after being elected one of the Managers of the Fund at its annual meeting, May 4th, 1852.

His services in this charity may be summed up thus: on the Committee of the Fund, one year; on the Committee of Relief, four years; on the Committee of Admission, ten years, or to the end of his days.

The share which Mr. Baldwin exercised in the political movements of the day, though limited in extent, were of much importance; he fulfilled the duties which they imposed upon him with his usual zeal and independence. As a member of the Convention to amend the Constitution of the State of Pennsylvania in 1837, he took, in that body, a decided stand on points that have become vital principles in the general progress or advance of the human race, and always on the side of liberality and justice.

Elected a member of the State legislature in 1853, he was distinguished, amid the mazes of diplomacy, during his term of service, in the winter of 1854, for his straightforward and consistent course in that line of conscientiousness which had marked his life.

As an Inspector of the County Prison, Mr. Baldwin may be cited as an example of persevering benevolence in an ungrateful task, marked by all the disagreeable and revolting feelings which accompany contact with the vile, the miserable, and the degraded.   In this office his sense of justice, and hatred of intemperance and vice in all its motley garb, must have been sorely tried; but mercy and benevolence seem to have been the prevailing sentiments which governed him in the treatment of the unfortunate and vicious with whom he came in contact in his inspection tours of duty.

It will be observed in the record of his career, as thus traced, that Mr. Baldwin was remarkable for the number and variety of the occupations and pursuits to which he devoted his working and his leisure hours; to do full justice to his character would require much more extended remarks (pleasant labor it is true), but not required by the objects of this notice.

His principal characteristic was the fervent religious bias of his mind; from early life it appears to have impressed him with its vital importance, and to have influenced him, more or less, in all the transactions of his career: it developed itself most forcibly in the aid which he gave to the formation of religious associations, and the building and support of churches, for that particular denomination to which he was attached; becoming more marked as he advanced in age, and as his means accumulated; so that his own revenue, great as it had become within the last few years of his business career, appears to have been almost absorbed in this direction.

That he was fond of everything beautiful in nature, is demonstrated by the flowers, the trees, and plants of his favorite residence at Wissinoming, which he had embellished to the utmost, in the fruits of the tropics, the vines and esculents of the most liberal horticulture, and all that constitute the surroundings of a refined life in the country. But his fondness was not confined to the vegetable kingdom alone; it led to the collection and guardianship of a variety of animals. The deer and other ruminants had their comfortable parks; the smaller animals their appropriate shelter; and every variety of bird, its home and sustenance; and some, too, were the pets of his lap, and seemed both the amusement and indulgence of a caressing habit of life.

His fondness for the fine arts was one of his characteristics; his houses and rooms were filled to their utmost capacity with the pictures which he paid for liberally and justly, but none of that extravagant ostentation in purchase prices which has been the wonder of latter days, had any footing in his well-selected collection. In this respect at least, his discrimination cannot be impeached.

The memorial of a man like this might well be a eulogy, but it may be also treated by a friend, impartially, and in full justice, without that extravagant praise which is so usual on such occasions. He was eminently social in his feelings and habits; at the same time, his principal characteristic was self-reliance; his own views, habits, and impulses, were those that he followed.

That his views on temperance were philanthropic, no one can doubt; but like all others holding ultra opinions, he found by experience that the laws of matter (by the ordination of Providence for its own wise purposes) cannot be resisted, and that fermentation and its products were intended by the Supreme Ruler, not for the abuse, but for the good of man.

His earnest endeavors to resist the fermentation of his abundant crop of grapes were of no avail, and the value of the products in medicine, suited to his own case, was ultimately recognized and admitted.

He was not a sportsman in any sense of the word, but it is equally true that he never appeared better pleased than when mounted on a fast horse, and sometimes an observant friend might see, if he looked sharply, that to let any ambitious roadster pass him was not usual, if possible. Neither can it be said that he was a gymnast; yet he habitually exercised his muscular system (recognizing its importance in hygiene), and contended with no little fervor for successful honors in that line; this was well known to his associates in the practice of archery.

His constitution was not robust; he suffered

much from ill health at various periods of his
life, the last years of which were years of suffering, more or less, but it never changed his kindly
feelings towards his friends, family, or the dumb
pets of his household; especially did it never
relax his energy in the great and complex business of his firm, or the more important charities
of his heart and purse.

Too much praise cannot be bestowed on the
final disposition of his worldly affairs; he did
all that he intended to do in charity and benevolence during life, and left to his heirs a bright
example for their guidance. In this respect, so
different from the ostentatious wording of those
testamentary dispositions that are now wasting
their ample provisions in political jugglery, or
turned aside by mismanagement to some other
object, perhaps more objectionable.

RESOLUTIONS

DEATH OF MATTHIAS W. BALDWIN.

28

RESOLUTIONS.

AT a meeting of the employees of the Works of M. W. Baldwin and Co., held September 10, 1866, Mr. James W. Blair was called to the chair, and Mr. R. A. Peirson appointed Secretary.

On motion, the following resolutions were adopted:—

WHEREAS, in the dispensation of that Almighty Father who ordereth all things for the best, one from amongst us, our late employer and friend, M. W. BALDWIN, Esq., has been called from the scene of his temporal labor, and bidden an everlasting farewell to the cares and trials of this earthly life, and it is proper that we should give expression to the feelings which so melancholy a bereavement is calculated to inspire: Therefore, be it

Resolved, That in adverting to the lamentable death, we cannot but bear in mind the purity and usefulness of his life, marked as it was by all those virtues which make men beautiful here below, that they may be better fitted for the glories of the hereafter.

Resolved, That his great character, as sincere as it was generous, acted like a charm upon all who came within its influence, and bound men to him in a firm and lasting friendship.

Resolved, That in simplicity of purpose, purity of intention, integrity of action, and goodness of heart, our employer was of the noblest works of God, an honest man; as such we knew him living, now mourn him dead.

Resolved, That a copy of these resolutions be presented to the family of the deceased, and likewise to the firm, and be published in all the daily papers.

Resolved, That we attend the funeral in a body.

> WM. S. HOSTER,
> THOS. BILLINGSFELT,
> WM. D. STRATTON,
> PETER FARNUM,   *Committee.*
> ROBT. CASSADIN,
> ROBT. ARMSTRONG,
> EDMUND BURKE,

Baldwin Locomotive Works,
Philada., Sept. 10*th,* 1866.

At a meeting of the foremen of these works, held this day, the following preamble and resolutions were adopted :—

Whereas, It has pleased Divine Providence to remove from our midst our friend and benefactor, Matthias W. Baldwin, Esq.; and

Whereas, While we bow with submission to the will of our Heavenly Father, we cannot but express our deep sorrow at being thus severed from one with whom we have been so long connected: Therefore be it

Resolved, That in the death of Matthias W. Baldwin, Esq., the community has lost a valuable member, his family a kind husband and father, and we a good friend, whose memory will ever be cherished in our hearts.

Resolved, That we tender to his family our warmest sympathies in their affliction, hoping they may be comforted with the assurance that his reward will be,

"Well done, thou good and faithful servant."

Resolved, That these resolutions be published

in the daily papers, and a copy transmitted to
the family of the deceased; and as a further mark
of respect, we attend the funeral in a body.

L. O. HOWELL, *President.*

Wm. Hobart Brown, *Secretary.*

———

PHILADELPHIA COUNTY PRISON,
Sept. 15, 1866.

At a meeting of the Board of Inspectors of
the Philadelphia County Prison, held September
10th, 1866, the following preamble and resolutions were offered by the Hon. Joseph R. Chan-
dler and *unanimously* adopted:—

Whereas, the members of the Board of Inspectors of the Philadelphia County Prison have
heard with profound regret the annunciation of
the death of their colleague, Matthias W.
Baldwin, Esq., and feel it due to the sterling
worth of the deceased, and to the cause of domestic, social, and public virtue which his whole
life so beautifully illustrated, to make a record of
their regard for his character, their appreciation

of his services as an associate, and their sorrow for his death.

In the various relations in which Mr. Baldwin stood to society, he manifested those qualities which attract attention and secure respect. His eulogists will find abundant materials for applause in the successful efforts with which he added to the credit and wealth of the city, while he secured to himself the means of that enlarged judicious liberality which connects his name with the highest acts and purest charities of Philadelphia.

It has been the privilege of the members of this Board to share the counsels of Mr. Baldwin in the discharge of duties devolved upon them by their appointment, and to witness his quiet, persistent efforts for the good of those whose errors or crimes make them involuntary inmates of this Prison, and testimony cordial and earnest is hereby borne to the unfailing urbanity, the steady justice, and the beautiful humanity which marked the course of the deceased as a member of this Board, and which make poignant and permanent the regret which his death has caused. It is therefore

Resolved, That this expression of deep regret

for the death of Mr. Baldwin and of profound respect for his memory, be entered at large upon the journal of the Board, and that an attested copy thereof be transmitted to the family of the deceased.

Resolved, That this Board will attend the funeral of their lately deceased member.

———

HALL FRANKLIN INSTITUTE,
Philadelphia.

AT a special meeting of the Board of Managers of the Franklin Institute, September 11th, 1866, the following preamble and resolutions were adopted:—

WHEREAS, MATTHIAS W. BALDWIN, one of the earliest members of the Franklin Institute, has, after a long and useful life, been separated by death from his family and friends: and

WHEREAS, the Managers of the Institute, cherishing a lively recollection of his services as a member, manager, and Vice-President, for many years; and also of the genius, skill, and industry which marked his career as a mechanic and manufacturer, deem it right to perpetuate on their records their high estimation of his character and worth: therefore—

Resolved, That it is with deep sorrow they have heard of the death of Mr. Baldwin, and of the severance of those earthly ties which for so many years bound him to the Institute and to its members in the cordial bonds of usefulness, personal friendship, and honorable competition in business, and in the promotion of the application of science to the useful arts.

Resolved, That we sincerely condole with his immediate family and friends in this great bereavement, and trust that the consoling remembrances of his pure and honest character, his Christian life and useful example to all men, may calm their sense of his loss, and lead them to that dependence on the source of all good, which so manifestly sustained him during his earthly career and made death the entrance to eternal life and happiness.

Resolved, That as a further mark of our affection and respect for our deceased friend and associate, we will in a body attend his funeral, and that the members of the Institute be re-

29

quested to join with us in paying this last tribute
to his memory.

Resolved, That a copy of the foregoing preamble and resolutions be sent to the family of
Mr. Baldwin by the President of the Institute.

BOARD OF TRUSTEES

OLIVET PRESBYTERIAN CHURCH,

Sept. 17th, 1866.

HAVING heard with sincere and deep sorrow
of the death of Matthias W. Baldwin, and being desirous at the first meeting since that event
of expressing our sense of the bereavement:
therefore

Resolved, First, That in view of the character
of the deceased, whose works testified to his
faith in the great Redeemer, and his love for
His cause, we find no ground of sorrow on his
own account for his removal from the earth.

Second, That in view of his pure morals, his
expanded principles, his warm patriotism, his
impartial benevolence, his large benefactions,
and exemplary Christian life, we express our

sense of the public loss and of the bereavement sustained by the Christian Church, especially by that denomination of which Mr. Baldwin was a member and ruling elder.

Third, That we claim the privilege of joining in the public expression of grief by reason of our large share in his Christian liberality, both when the church was first organized and in the late attempts to enlarge her accommodations for worship. His liberal donation has enabled us to erect a House of God commodious and convenient, which we doubt not will remain for generations to come a place for receiving saving spiritual good, and this record is intended to keep alive in the hearts of our people a grateful remembrance of him who has now been called to the "better country."

Fourth, That we hereby express our lively sympathy with the bereaved family, acknowledging at the same time that our warmest expressions are a small alleviation for the loss of one so kind, so good, so provident, and so closely endeared; whose loss in the family circle must be irreparable, except as God shall make it good.

At a meeting of the Executive Committee of the Ministerial Relief Fund, held in the Presbyterian House, Sept. 18, 1866, the following paper was unanimously adopted:—

"Whereas, it pleased the Lord, on the 7th of September, 1866, to remove from us by death, Matthias W. Baldwin, Esq., of Philadelphia:

"And Whereas, Mr. Baldwin, from the first, was a member of the Executive Committee of the Ministerial Relief Fund: therefore

"*Resolved*, That while we bow with Christian submission to this sad dispensation, we would record our high appreciation of Mr. Baldwin as one of the most excellent among men, and a bright example in every department of usefulness. We also deplore the heavy loss which has befallen us in his removal from our earthly associations, to enter the everlasting rest which God prepared for him in heaven."

PHILADELPHIA, *Sept.* 19, 1866.

AT the stated meeting of the Pennsylvania Horticultural Society, held last evening, the following resolutions, offered by Mr. Caleb Cope, were unanimously adopted :—

Resolved, That this Society records with the profoundest sorrow the death of one of its Vice-Presidents, Matthias W. Baldwin, who for many years was a most attentive and useful member of this institution, and during a considerable portion of the time its able, courteous, and dignified presiding officer.

Resolved, That this Society will ever bear in grateful remembrance the valuable services rendered to it, and through it to the public, by reason of the many interesting contributions furnished by Mr. Baldwin from his extensive conservatories on the Delaware, the more especially for his liberal subscription to the Building fund, without which the present effort to erect a Hall for the uses of the Society would not be made.

Resolved, That whilst this Society deeply mourns over its own bereavement, it deplores also the loss which many other institutions, churches, and individuals experience in the death of so estimable a citizen, who illustrated a long life by the most munificent gifts, noble enterprises, and the observance of a uniform, urbane, and truly Christian deportment.

Resolved, That whilst no words can adequately express, and no acts sufficiently indicate the fraternal attachment of the surviving members of this Society to their departed and lamented friend, they will take early measures to procure a portrait of him, that it may adorn those walls he had so materially aided to erect, trusting that each spectator who may be favored to look upon it in future years, may alike revere the memory of the original, and endeavor to imitate his bright example.

Resolved, That the pervading sadness visible in the countenances of those assembled in this Hall to-night, notwithstanding there is much in the collected beautiful productions of nature otherwise calculated to gladden and cheer, shows how universal is the regret among those who have for so many years witnessed the splendid specimens of Horticulture which Mr. Baldwin has so generously exposed to public view at the meetings of the Society, and also in his elegant conservatory on Chestnut Street, which was erected and supplied for the benefit of that public exclusively.

Resolved, That a copy of these proceedings, signed by the President and Secretary, be presented to the immediate family of the deceased, accompanied by the assurance that this Society most deeply sympathizes with the members thereof in the great calamity that has befallen them.

PHILADELPHIA, *Sept.* 25, 1866.

THE Board of Directors of Horticultural Hall have heard with the profoundest sorrow of the decease of their late colleague and friend, Matthias W. Baldwin, and have directed me to present to the family of the departed the assurance of their high esteem for him as a man, as a public benefactor, as a truly Christian gentleman, whom all honored and all mourned.

When a good man dies, all men grieve.

With high respect,

A. W. HARRISON, *Rec. Sec'ry.*

To the family of the late M. W. BALDWIN.

PENNSYLVANIA ACADEMY OF THE FINE ARTS,
PHILADELPHIA, *October* 1st, 1866.

AT a stated meeting of the Board of Managers, held this day, the following preamble and resolutions were presented by Franklin Peale:—

WHEREAS: In assembling on this occasion, we are made conscious of the vacancy in this body by the decease of Matthias W. Baldwin, so long a member of it; whose presence has always been recognized as an able and reliable aid in the affairs of the institution; and his departure as a loss of no ordinary character.

He became a member of the Board at the annual election of 1852, and served on various Committees, particularly that of Finance, in which capacity he rendered efficient services until his decease, which took place at Wissinoming, his suburban residence, on the 7th of September, 1866, in the seventy-first year of his age.

We therefore deem it our duty to place on the records of the Academy a brief but expressive notice of the estimation in which he was held as one of its managers, together with our consideration of him as a member of the community at large; a patron of the Fine Arts, and a liberal and just man.

Be it therefore Resolved, That the Board accept these remarks as a deserved tribute to his memory, and a just though faint expression of the esteem in which he was held as their associate and fellow-citizen.

Be it further Resolved, That this preamble and resolutions be inserted on the Minutes of the Academy as a permanent record of our sentiments, and that a copy of them, signed by the President and Secretary, be transmitted to the family of our late associate, in evidence of our sympathy on this melancholy occasion.

———

RESOLUTIONS adopted by the Calvary Church Session, at their first meeting after Mr. Baldwin's decease, held October 17, 1866.

Resolved, That in the death of our late beloved brother and highly esteemed elder, Matthias W. Baldwin, we feel that we have met with a loss which seems irreparable, and which fills us with the deepest sorrow.

30

That, while we reverently submit to the will of God in this afflictive event, we desire to record our sense of the high value of his counsels, example, and influence as a member of this session, and of this church since its organization; and also to express our gratitude to God for the deeds of beneficence and piety which have distinguished our brother in this city and almost throughout Christendom.

Resolved, That we hereby tender to the bereaved. and sorrowing family of our lamented brother our Christian sympathy and our sincere condolence, and also assure them that our earnest prayer is, that the wisdom and grace which guided him in life, and the faith and hope which sustained him in death, may be their all-sufficient support and comfort in this day of grief and affliction.

That the Clerk be requested to send a copy of these resolutions to Mrs. Baldwin.

CALVARY CHURCH SUNDAY SCHOOL,

PHILADELPHIA, *December* 3*d*, 1866.

WHEREAS, The Almighty Disposer of events, who giveth life and taketh it away as seemeth

to Him good, has removed from among us Mr.
Matthias W. Baldwin, who has presided over
the interests of our Sunday School as Superintendent from its organization until his death:

Resolved, That we, the officers and teachers of
the Sunday School he loved, recognize and endeavor to bow submissively to the Providence
which has thus afflicted us, feeling confident
that one who labored so earnestly in The Master's cause has not failed to find that "to be with
Christ is far better" than even the joy of doing
good on the earth.

Resolved, That we will always cherish the
memory of our late Superintendent as one who
in childlike simplicity and earnest faith, with an
ever constant sense of the presence of God, and
of his dependence on Him, endeavored to be a
faithful steward of the Lord's bounties, and to
exemplify in his daily walk and conversation
the spirit of our holy religion.

Resolved, That though our school and the
church of which we form a part have suffered
a loss which seems to us irreparable in the removal of Mr. Baldwin, we remember the blow
has fallen more heavily upon those who mourn
a husband and a father dead, and we desire to

express our heartfelt sympathy with them, and give utterance to the prayer that his God may be their support and consolation in this their great sorrow.

Resolved, That these resolutions be entered upon the Minutes of the Association, and that a copy of the same be sent to the family of the deceased.

B. Kendall,	M. K. Nassau,
Jno. R. Neff,	J. S. Erskine,
Samuel Mercer,	Kate B. Patton,
S. W. Colton, Jr.,	Mary E. Ashman,
D. C. McCammon,	Clara Redfield,
Jno. H. Williams,	Eliza Cornwall,
S. Henry Norris,	Lizzie S. Dale,
John A. Lewis,	Mrs. E. A. Groves,
Henry N. Paul,	A. M. Strong,
Wm. B. Leidy,	Anna C. McElroy,
M. L. Frederick,	Elizabeth E. Frost,
Robert N. Willson,	Emily Judson,
A. McElroy,	M. H. Frederick,
John H. Atwood,	Mary S. Otto,
Charles Stewart Wurts,	Sarah Scattergood,
Emily E. Strong,	H. M. Wurts.
E. A. White,	

AT a meeting of the Trustees of the Presbyterian House, held in the House Wednesday, December 5th, A. D. 1866—

"The death of Matthias W. Baldwin, Esquire, a Trustee of the House, was announced; whereupon, it was

"*Resolved*, That the Trustees record, with profound sorrow, their sense of the loss thus sustained, to themselves, to the denomination, and to the church at large. They deplore the removal from themselves of a genial and generous co-laborer; from the denomination, of a faithful and honored elder; from the church at large, of a Christian whose liberality to all good enterprises was as princely as his piety was simple and sincere. They recognize, in the death of their late associate, the monitory exhortation 'to do with their might what their hands find to do.'"